PRAISE FOR THE STIG SERIES

' ..t-paced and funny' *Sunday Times*

'..e again the second book in The Stig series is another fast-...d adventure with lots of mystery, action and humour. ..horter chapters mean the story zips along. Fantastic for ...;er readers and fans of cars and *Top Gear*. My students ...) can't wait for the third book'
..na Suffield, School Librarian of the Year 2018

'..e action rattles along at a rate of knots with twists and turns ..very corner . . . at the sight of the book, I had a queue of ..s in my class wanting to borrow it. Five stars'
..ingzone.com

'..st-paced action story featuring cars, computer games, an ..illionaire, racing tournaments and of course, The Stig. ..ppeal will be obvious to some readers, but even readers ..o experience of *Top Gear* can quickly become absorbed .. page-turning adventure full of twists and turns'
CP/494 **..fortopics.com**

'A great book for getting kids off those screens and into regular reading!' **n**

AND THE
SILVER GHOST

The Stig series

**The Stig Plays a
Dangerous Game**

The Stig Drives Again

**The Stig and
the Silver Ghost**

Look out for more
from The Stig

THE STIG

AND THE SILVER GHOST

JON CLAYDON & TIM LAWLER

Piccadilly PRESS

First published in Great Britain in 2019 by
PICCADILLY PRESS
80–81 Wimpole St, London W1G 9RE
www.piccadillypress.co.uk

A CIP catalogue record for this book is available from the British Library.

ISBN: 978-1-84812-671-8
Also available as an ebook

1

This book is typeset by James Fraser
Printed and bound in Great Britain by Clays Ltd, Elcograf S.p.A.

Piccadilly Press is an imprint of Bonnier Books UK
www.bonnierbooks.co.uk

For
James, Edie and Daniel

Some say he's the opposite of the Mona Lisa.
No matter where you're standing
in the room, he still ignores you.

All we know is . . .

PROLOGUE

Christmas Eve, late afternoon

Dr David Evans drove his Land Rover Discovery with care along the frozen main road towards Bunsfold.

'Ding Dong Merrily On High' played quietly in the background, for the second time that evening. He'd now listened to each of the *World's Favourite Carols* at least once.

Alongside him his wife Deborah sat with head tilted back, eyes closed and mouth half open. In the back, Tom – sixteen last week – and Becky – ten and three quarters – sat glued to their phone screens. Behind them was a small hillock of Christmas presents piled high in the boot. They were en route to David's parents' home, the modest house on Harris Drive where he'd spent an uneventful childhood.

'Are we nearly there?' asked Becky.

'Ten minutes,' he replied.

'Fifteen,' muttered his wife, waking up.

They'd disagreed – as usual – on which route to take and, being the driver, he'd won. But now he'd elected to sidestep any further disputes by appointing the car's satnav to guide them the last few miles.

'In two hundred and fifty yards, turn left.'

 1

'Okay, Team Evans,' said the doctor. 'Chat to me. It *is* Christmas, after all.'

Tom yanked his headphones off.

'Great!' he said, with sarcastic enthusiasm. 'What'll we talk about, Dad? Why not tell us *one more time* about how you fell off your bike in Bunsfold Woods?'

'Tom, what exactly is your problem?'

The boy stared out of the window. 'No idea. Maybe it's something to do with having to spend Christmas in the most boring place in the universe. *Again.*'

'Bunsfold? Oh, it's not boring,' said the doctor. 'Trust me.'

'No, Dad, you're right,' said his son. 'It's a seething hotbed of glamour and adventure.'

'Tom,' said his mother, 'enough.'

'There's more to sleepy Bunsfold than meets the eye,' said the doctor. 'Strange things have happened here.'

'What kind of strange things?' said Becky.

'Visions. Sightings. Hauntings.'

'Don't forget the alien abductions,' said Tom. 'That's what you get when you build a village on the site of Surrey's only known Apache burial ground.'

The doctor caught his son's eye in the mirror.

'Have I ever told you about the witch in the woods?'

'No!' said Becky, perking up.

'An eyeless crone that terrorised the village in the seventeenth century,' said her dad, now enjoying the attention. 'Due to reappear this very year.'

His wife turned to him to shoot a 'where are you going with this, exactly?' sort of look.

'The Bunsfold Witch,' said Dr Evans. 'She lived in these woods exactly four hundred years ago.'

'If possible,' interrupted the satnav, *'make a U-turn.'*

'Who was she?' said Becky.

'A single woman with a cat, probably,' said her mum. 'People were just very superstitious back then.'

'Don't tell me,' said her brother. 'She'd turn up at midnight to steal away naughty children that hadn't done enough revision.'

'Half right,' said the doctor. 'She *did* abduct children.'

'In four hundred yards, take the second exit,' piped up the satnav.

'I don't believe it,' groaned the doctor. 'It's sending us the long way round.'

'Through the woods?' said Becky. 'Where the witch lived?'

'Better lock the doors just in case, eh?' said Tom.

A thick fog had descended, making the going even slower than before. The doctor turned on his lights.

'What do you mean,' said Becky, 'abduct children?'

'She'd lure them to the very edge of the woods with irresistible treats,' said the doctor. 'Meat pies, I think.'

'Okaaay . . .' said Tom, finally intrigued.

'Then, just when they'd reach over for a slice – BANG! She'd bag them and whisk them into the woods, never to be seen again.'

'I can't believe you just said that,' said his wife. 'Dad's joking, kids.'

'Well, one thing is true,' said the doctor. 'It's exactly four hundred years since she was killed off, and this year Bunsfold is celebrating . . . a *Black Christmas*.'

'Wow,' said Becky. 'What's that?'

'No one knows for sure, but it seems it's quite special. I can't wait to see what. . .'

'Abstinence Barebones!' proclaimed Tom, eyes shining in the reflected light of his phone. 'That was her name! "The Witch of Bunsfold". Dad, you're right! She was in charge of the children at the workhouse on the hill, but instead of looking after them she . . . stole them away. "Believed responsible for the deaths of sixteen children . . . two-year reign of terror . . . black magic . . . witchcraft . . ." All sorts. Says here she made their right arms into . . .'

He stopped, and glanced at Becky.

'Anyway, she was executed exactly four hundred years ago, leaving a curse on the village and swearing to return "after four centuries had passed and darkness once more stalked the earth, for . . ."'

'Thanks, Tom,' said his mum. 'That'll do.'

'. . . vengeance,' finished Tom, quietly.

'And on that bombshell,' said his mum, determined to change the subject, 'time to answer the burning question of the night. Who gets the last purple Quality Street?'

Soon everything was back to normal – apart from the fog,

which was getting even thicker. The kids had snuck their headphones back on and Mrs E's eyes were closed once more.

The traffic had disappeared now, and the road was dark. Trees arched overhead, blocking any moonlight that might otherwise have struggled through the fog. And then:

'At the next junction, turn left.'

He guided the Land Rover, as instructed, onto what looked more like a mud track than a road.

Not ideal.

But the voice in the dashboard had another instruction for him.

'Then come unto me, boy . . . Thou art a flesh-monger.'

He jolted upright, and froze.

'What the . . . ? DEBORAH!'

His wife started awake and turned to him, alarmed.

'Are you okay? You look like death.'

'The satnav! I could have the sworn it just . . .' He composed himself. 'Sorry. Forget it. Must be more tired than I thought.'

'Dad,' said Becky, 'I *really* don't like this road. Can we sit in the traffic jam instead?'

She had a point. The route the satnav had chosen was narrow, winding, muddy – and now completely shrouded in thick mist. Where on earth were they heading?

'In one hundred yards, you will arrive at your destination . . .'

And then something very strange happened.

The satnav . . . chuckled.

A single, scratchy, dry-throated cackle. No doubt about it.

'David,' said Deb calmly, 'did you hear that?'

He stopped the car.

'We're more than a hundred yards from Mum and Dad's place, that's for sure,' he said. 'This thing's sending us . . . somewhere else.'

He glanced in the rear-view mirror, to check if reversing was an option. But backing up over a mile in the dark? In these conditions?

'Where are we?' said his wife quietly.

'Dad,' said Becky, 'I want to go home.'

'The pastry's warm,' said the satnav. *'Now for the meat.'*

'Oh God . . . !' shrieked Deborah. 'Where's this coming from?'

'Lock the doors!' ordered the doctor.

'You have now arrived at your destination,' said the satnav.

Then . . .

'I confess myself an object of God's loathing.'

The fog engulfed the car. They could see nothing. Tom reached for his mobile.

'I'm calling for help . . . Grandpa? The police?'

His phone beeped.

He had a text.

He screamed, and hurled the phone to the floor.

'What's wrong? What is it?'

Deborah reached back, picked up the mobile and read the message.

I CAN SEE YOU, TOM EVANS.

The phone beeped a second time.

I'M OUTSIDE YOUR WINDOW, YOU SEE.

Then a third.

I'LL DRAIN YOU FIRST.

'Dad!' cried Tom. 'Get us out of here! PLEASE!'

A shrivelled, bony hand slammed against the side window.

A gnarled finger began to write.

'I'M . . . BACK.'

FIRST

BUNSFOLD, A DAY EARLIER
Ford Harrison takes a test

The boy's hair was spiky, all right. In her career as a Child Assessor, Ms Bluegrass had seldom seen spikier. She'd also seldom seen grades anything like this. She wouldn't say the child's exam papers were the most terrible she'd seen, but they were in the top one.

'I've been looking forward to meeting you, Ford,' she said. 'The boy whose results cover the entire range of marks between zero and one per cent. That one point was achieved by spelling your name correctly at the top of the geography paper.'

'Lucky guess,' muttered the boy.

'Yet when it came to the examinations themselves, you managed total consistency. Not a single question answered correctly, and most not answered at all.' She raised an eyebrow. 'Such a performance would generally see a child transferred to a school for the academically challenged. Many thrive in them. I've seen some amazing work with coloured bricks.'

The boy just sat, a prickly urchin on a beach of boredom.

'The previous headmaster insisted there was a functioning

brain beneath those spikes, but your current teachers disagree. So let's find out who's right. We'll start with a simple word-association test. I say a word, you say the first thing that comes into your head. So, for example, I might say "black", and you might reply "white". Ready?'

'Steady,' said the boy. 'Next?'

'No, that wasn't a word,' said the adult.

'Pretty sure it was.'

The woman paused before continuing.

'Tomato.'

'Tomato,' said the boy.

'That's right. So, what word comes to mind when I say tomato?'

'Tomato.'

'No, what *other* word?'

'What's wrong with my word?'

'It can't be the same thing that I said.'

'Why not?'

'It just can't. Let's try again. *Tomato.'*

'Different tomato.'

Ms Bluegrass sighed inwardly. Her last assessment of the year was hardly a Christmas cracker. She knew only too well that the chances of a child like Ford Harrison – single parent, bad attitude, academically backward – ever really *making* something of himself were slim at best.

She continued. 'I have all day, you know. And we're not leaving here until . . .'

'Okay, okay,' said the boy. He picked up a pencil and began tapping it lightly on the desk.

Ms Bluegrass took a deep breath and tried again.

'Man.'

'Cruiser.'

She nodded, as if to say *hmm, interesting,* and made a note on her pad.

'Woman.'

'Battle.'

Ms Bluegrass couldn't suppress a tiny gasp.

'What's wrong?'

'Most children say dad and mum, that's all.'

'Why?'

'Because that's what comes to mind. Whereas you associate the adult female with conflict.'

'Trust me. If you'd ever met *this* adult female, so would you.'

She made another note, then continued.

'Family.'

'Overrated.'

'Father.'

'Mystery.'

'Dog.'

'Pizza.'

Ms Bluegrass's cheeks reddened.

'Seriously,' said Ford. 'That's what popped into my head. I could explain why, but I'm not sure you'd . . . Look, shall we just pretend I said "cat"?'

She made another note and resumed.

'*Storm.*'

'Coming.'

'*Bad.*'

'Cruisers.'

'*White.*'

'Shark.'

'*Dead.*'

The boy paused. Then, softly:

'Stig.'

Ms Bluegrass looked up crossly. 'All right. What, exactly, is a "Stig"?'

'Interesting question, Ms Bluegrass. The truth is, no one's quite sure.' He paused. 'Some say . . .'

He caught the look of cold impatience on the face of his assessor.

'Can I change my answer? Let's go with "alive". Are we done now? Can I go?'

His assessor continued writing on her pad, making a point of not looking up until she was good and ready.

A distant *dubdubdubdub* from outside broke the silence.

That's odd, thought Ford. *Why would a Russian Mi-26 'Halo' transport helicopter be hovering above Bunsfold?* He glanced out of the window but saw nothing: just a low, dense fog. Strange.

His phone beeped.

'*Caller ID withheld.*' Interesting. He read the message.

'MEET BCHQ. 11.30. CODE RED.'

'Miss, are we done?' he said, pushing back his chair. 'Only I've gotta go –'

'Sit DOWN!' interrupted Ms Bluegrass.

Ford slumped on to the chair again.

The assessor leaned back and arched her fingers, bringing the tips together.

'Mr Harrison. I'm not sure you realise how serious your situation is. You're about to be removed from Bunsfold High altogether, to somewhere more appropriate to your abilities. Away from your home. Away from your school. Away from your . . . gang.'

Ford sat up like a spiky meerkat who'd just heard a howl, disturbingly nearby.

'Good. I see I finally have your attention. Until I see some evidence of a functioning brain, young man, you will be going absolutely *nowhere.*'

Silence.

'Now. The final word is . . .'

She gave a fake smile so wide it almost met around the back of her head.

'*Sunshine.*'

'A portion of the electromagnetic radiation emitted by the sun,' replied Ford, gazing out of the window. 'Our closest star emits radiation across most of the electromagnetic spectrum, but the only direct signature of the nuclear process is the emission of neutrinos. This life-giving force was often worshipped as a god by early hominids but these days is more often enjoyed under sunscreen with a good book on a . . . Pencil ready?'

And he turned to fix her with a stare so intense, it pinned her to her chair.

'. . . beach.'

The assessor's lips were now as thin as a stray hair.

'Mr Harrison,' she said, 'why do you pretend to be dim?'

'The same reason, Ms Bluegrass, you pretend to be nice,' said Ford, rising from his chair. 'So they don't see me coming.'

There wasn't a breath deep enough for her to take.

SECOND

In which an ominous helicopter
moves into position over Bunsfold

Sam Wheeler, Surrey under-13s downhill mountain biking champion, had been looking forward to this ride. Buster Mustang, holder of a good few biking titles of his own, was over from the USA for the holidays.

The time had come to settle an issue they'd been dancing around for quite some time. Who was quicker on a bike?

So, that crisp, Christmassy morning, they'd arranged to meet at Sam's house for the shootout. First to the Den – also known as 'BCHQ' – wins. There were no other rules.

Buster had brought TG Dog along to referee. Sam's ancient grandfather was delighted to see the scruffy mutt again, and the dog clearly felt the same; so much so that Sam started to worry. Just how hard can a panting pooch lick an elderly war hero's hand before the skin wears through?

'Last one there's a hippy-haired Brit,' said Buster, as Sam emerged from the house wearing . . . What the heck was *that*?

It looked like one of those huge inflatable sumo suits you sometimes get at parties. In a fetching hi-vis orange.

'Hate to break it,' said Buster, stifling a giggle, 'but pumpkin costumes passed their wear-by date two months ago.'

He looked at Gramps, who was biting his sleeve in a valiant effort not to laugh.

'Okay, okay,' said Sam. 'Mum made me promise. Small price to pay for staying safe, she says.'

'Looks a pretty high price to me,' said Buster. 'So does it inflate further on impact, or light up, or sing your dreary national anthem, or what?'

'It's an airbag, so of course it inflates,' said Sam, as if it was the most normal thing in the world. 'Now, are we talking or racing?'

'Oh, don't worry, Captain Teletubby, we're racing,' said Buster. 'And you're going *down*. All the way to Laa-Laa Land.'

Gramps prepared to start the race, before pausing wistfully for a moment.

'I envy you boys,' he said. TG cocked her head and paid him the kind of attention usually reserved for people opening tins. 'Yes, and girls too,' he said with a pat. 'I've had gangs in my time. They're all gone now, of course, and won't be coming back. But yours is up there with the best. Enjoy it while you can. I've been rich and I've been poor; talked to prime ministers and traffic wardens; even learned a lesson or two. But looking back over a long, long haul, I've discovered one thing for sure. *Nothing* beats a proper gang of mates, like you, that have each other's backs.'

Sam suddenly looked a bit emotional. As always, Buster had his back.

'Well, then,' he said, 'you'll just have to join *ours*. We were only saying the other day how we could do with a bit of experience in the team, weren't we, Samwise?'

'Absolutely,' said Sam firmly. 'Someone with a few thousand hours' flying time, we thought.'

'Zippy on a Zimmer,' said Buster.

'Stellar on a stairlift,' added Sam. 'Anyone spring to mind?'

Gramps smiled, the hint of a glisten visible behind the thick lenses of his spectacles. 'Honoured to serve, sir.' He stood to attention and saluted them both.

'At ease, Squadron Leader,' said Sam. 'And welcome to the Top Gear Gang.'

'Good. So now *that's* settled,' said Buster, turning to Sam, 'it's down to business. You. In the mango-suit. We racing or what?'

Gramps took his cue. 'This is not a drill,' he said, producing an ancient RAF pistol. But before he raised it in the air, the old man paused.

'Be careful out there today, boys,' he said, gazing into the distance. 'There's something in the air. Something . . . odd.'

'Spidey-senses tingling, huh?' said Buster.

'Don't know about spiders, but mine certainly are,' said Gramps. 'And I've learned to trust 'em. Keep your wits about you. Something's not . . . right.'

Gramps fired into the air and they shot off. He watched until they disappeared from view – then shook his head clear of the vague sense of worry that had bothered him all morning.

The boys raced to the end of Sam's road, through town and onwards, neck-and-neck all the way up the lung-bursting climb at the edge of Bunsfold.

Then they paused, as always, at the gates of the brooding Mansion on the Hill, once home to evil dillionaire PT Cruiser, would-be enslaver of the human race and general rotten egg.

Deserted houses sometimes look sad. This one looked bad. It glowered down at them, pitch-black windows seeming to follow their every move like so many eyeless sockets. *Come and have a go,* it seemed to say, *if you think you're hard enough.*

Above the entrance loomed a huge stone pineapple, one of a pair, that had loomed there since anyone could remember. The other had toppled off, giving the house a lopsided look that somehow added to the menace.

'Why,' said Buster, panting, 'is it always pineapples?'

'Because,' said Sam, 'bananas would look silly.'

'Fair point,' said Buster. 'And there's its pal.'

Propped against the mansion's high enclosing wall was a huge pile of derelict mansion-junk, among which two especially large items rather dominated. A giant stone pineapple with some chunks missing, and the burnt-out chassis of a car.

But not just any car.

'If I'm not mistaken,' said Sam, who never was when it came to cars, 'that was once an *actual* Chrysler PT Cruiser.'

'You mean,' said Buster, 'the rubbish concept car that went on to become a totally pants nineties family hatchback?'

'The same,' said Sam. 'And here it is, burnt out and washed

up. Almost as if someone was making a point.'

'Yeah,' said Buster, 'real poetic. Now, talking of making points . . . Game . . . back . . . ON!'

They raced away, keen to get out of the mansion's sight-line, until Buster suddenly once more skidded to a halt.

'Incoming,' he said, pointing at the sky.

It was the *batabatabata* sound of a distant helicopter. High up, but obviously huge.

TG growled up at it as it flew overhead, almost falling over backwards in the process.

'Chinook?' said Sam, as he had a vague idea those were rather large.

'Duh,' said Buster. 'Single rotor. Nope, looks like a Halo to me.'

'Of course. A Halo, 'said Sam, nodding wisely. 'And that would be . . . ?'

'NATO codename for the Russian Mil Mi-26, largest helicopter ever. Been the heavyweight champ for a while now. Can take off with twice its own weight and travel for . . . Am I boring you?'

'Yes,' said Sam. 'But you had me right up until NATO.'

'What can I say?' protested Buster. 'When your pa's in the forces, you get to know the hardware. So what's *your* top Russian chopper?'

'So many to choose from,' sighed Sam. 'I think I'd have to go with . . . the Not-a-Clue-Vitch Whirl-Whirlski GT.'

'Interesting choice,' said Buster, straight-faced. 'Question is, what's this one doing here? You only use them to carry something BIG.'

'Presents,' said Sam. 'Obviously.'

They watched the departing chopper until it was almost invisible, shrouded in a fast-descending fog.

'Let's go,' said Buster. 'Weather's on the turn.'

Just then, their phones beeped simultaneously.

'*Caller ID withheld*,' read Sam aloud. 'MEET BCHQ. 11.30. CODE RED.'

'What's a code red?' said Buster, frowning.

'No idea,' said Sam. 'But by coincidence, BCHQ's exactly where we're headed. Three . . . two . . .'

He sped off, Buster and dog in hot pursuit.

'One,' said Sam, grinning to himself.

He *totally* had this.

THIRD

*In which a sinister fog
descends on the town*

Cabriola Cruiser woke around 10 a.m., stretched her long limbs, sat up and . . . *Ow*. Of course, she remembered, rubbing her head: no more cathedral-sized bedrooms for her. Lesson learned.

While her evil dillionaire relatives were sampling the catering in maximum-security prisons, Cabriola found herself back in good old Bunsfold, having accepted Mrs Harrison's kind offer to stay with her, Ford and Buster, over for the holidays.

A dose of 'normal' was just what she needed. Anyway, she had nowhere else to go.

She sat up and wiped away a tear. It was the same nightmare, every night. Watching her friend and protector, the late Maurice Marina, falling away from her into the abyss. Every time, she'd reach out to grab his outstretched hand. Every time, she'd miss.

He'd been the only person in the world who really knew her: a hard case with a soft heart. Not many girls could boast a mother-substitute who could bench-press 300 pounds. And while she felt more like an orphan than ever, he was with her still. She'd had her best conversations with him since he'd died.

She shook away one final, bitter tear. What use is knowing someone will sacrifice his life for you, if he actually does? It's like keeping the guarantee and throwing away the product.

Now she had no family at all.

Snap out of it, Cabriola Cruiser. Two more sleeps to the big day. Presents to wrap, mince pies to scoff, phone chargers to argue over. Normality!

And the gang was back together – which, thought Cab with a shiver of anticipation, usually signalled something interesting. Probably dangerous, too. She began to wonder if she'd become addicted.

Though Mrs H had insisted on one condition. 'No more of all this saving-the-world nonsense, thank you. We've had quite enough of that already this year.'

Right, rise and shine. She opened the attic curtains. A crisp winter day: just what the elves ordered.

Up in the sky, far off, she glimpsed a heavy helicopter, over where her pop's old house had been. She winced. Helicopters hadn't always been a happy omen in her past, and as for the mansion . . .

Still. All that was behind her now. And for once, she was home alone. Mrs H had taken Ford to some appointment, Buster had biked over to Sam's and she had the run of the house. Woo-hoo.

First up was a sneaky shower in Mrs H's bathroom, blissfully free of products aimed at twelve-year-old boys – Sports Prowess deodorant; Power Spike hair gel; White Fang toothpaste. And

Special Duty, an antiperspirant 'especially formulated for the committed gamer.' *Eeeaoww.*

How lovely to spend the morning in a room smelling of actual fragrances rather than pheromones and moose. And what a pleasure to enjoy a *proper* loofah, unlike the monstrosity she'd accidently used in the boys' shower. Which, to be fair, had turned out to be Buster's baseball mitt hanging up to dry.

Once dressed – jeans, camo hoody and a light dusting of Twilight Insolence body spray – she bounced downstairs and into the kitchen.

She would *totally* ace this 'making your own breakfast' thing. She'd been known to save worlds before breakfast. How hard could it be?

Start with something easy. An egg. She picked one from the basket by the cooker, found the eggcups and settled down at the table. She'd watched her personal chef prepare them dozens of times. You take the spoon, remove the top and it looks . . . *nothing* like that. There's runny, and there's Usain Bolt.

I get it, she thought. *Someone has to cook it first.* And these days, that someone was her. Talk about a faff. Wait. Microwave! She located the machine, placed the whole egg inside and turned the timer.

Just then, there was a message alert from her phone.

'*Caller ID withheld.*' Interesting. She read the message.

'MEET BCHQ. 11.30. CODE RED.'

The only problem was, she had no idea what a code red might be.

Cab felt her pulse quicken. It seemed the game was afoot.

She peeked outside. A thick and rather sinister fog had descended. She shuddered. Nerves? Or excitement? She sometimes found it hard to tell.

Yes, she thought as she strode towards the door.

Definitely addicted.

FOURTH

In which we learn about Abstinence
Barebones, the Bunsfold Witch.

The boys were neck-and-neck as they approached the halfway point in the middle of town. TG Dog bounded alongside, keeping a sharp doggy eye out for ungentlemanly conduct. But when they saw the scene in the foggy town square, all three stopped dead.

This was *weird*.

There was the expected tall pine tree in the middle, but it was hung with moons and dark stars rather than colourful baubles. At the top sat not a fairy but a witch: black hat, green face and a worryingly wicked wink.

The churchyard always housed a nativity scene, but this year's was disturbingly different. A huddle of dark cloaks surrounded the spot where the crib or manger might be. Instead of docile donkeys looking on, there were three outsized black cats. And where the waxwork shepherds should have stood, a row of broomsticks leaned against the wall as if proposing earwigs, dust and spiders' webs as birthday gifts.

Above this strange scene hung a banner with old-time writing saying:

What did *that* mean?

'What does that mean?' panted Buster. 'Ours at home mainly say *Happy Holidays*. And what's with all the black?'

He froze.

The huddle around the manger began to move.

Not waxworks after all, then.

The boys were transfixed as four hoods turned to face them, to reveal . . . nothing. Just black. No eyes. No faces.

Maybe it was the fog. Or maybe something spookier. The boys cycled on without a word. Whatever was going on, getting away from it seemed like a fine idea.

TG gave a low growl as one of the huge cats began to follow them – then a loud yelp as the others did the same.

'It's okay, girl,' said Buster, stroking her head. 'Just three adults in giant black cat costumes. Nothing remotely unusual.'

They cycled away slowly until they passed the old-fashioned toyshop where, what seemed like centuries ago, Sam had once bought a ball. Over the door were the usual faded letters: TOYS-GAMES-SPORTS. But instead of the wooden yachts and board games, the window contained one very prominent sign:

DING, DONG, THE WITCH IS BACK!
BUT ONLY FOR A SPELL

– SO TAKE ADVANTAGE WHILE YOU CAN OF OUR BLACK CHRISTMAS OFFERS!

'*Black* Christmas?' read Buster. 'What's that?'

'Local legend,' said Sam. 'Abstinence Barebones was known as the Bunsfold Witch, and she's meant to return after four hundred years or something. Executed on Christmas Eve, I think, and this year's the anniversary . . . Am I boring you?'

Buster was looking over his shoulder.

'Absolutely,' said Buster. Then, to someone else: 'Pretty nuts, huh?'

A girl aged around ten had appeared beside them, looking at the sign. Pale summer dress, cardigan with a hole in one sleeve. She turned to reveal a pleasant face with pale blue eyes. Her hair was so blonde it was almost silver.

'Nice outfit,' she said to Sam, glancing at his mango-suit.

'Er . . . thanks,' he replied warily. 'Aren't you cold?'

'No,' she said. Then, after a pause, 'Be careful in the fog.'

'Yeah, pretty scary, huh?' teased Buster, smiling.

'You have no idea,' replied the girl, not smiling back.

'Well, merry, um, Blackmas!' said Buster, shooting off towards the rec.

TG Dog looked up at the girl, head cocked to one side, and did a sort of doggy bow. The girl gave a sort of bow back. TG bounded off after Buster.

'He means Merry Christmas,' said Sam. 'My friend. Not the dog.'

'She means it too,' said the girl.

Sam set off after Buster. Not having a sister, and no reason to talk to younger girls like, ever, he wasn't sure if they all sounded like that. But this one seemed way different from the other kids back in KS2.

He caught up with Buster and TG at the recreation ground, where they were waiting to resume the race. The rec was full of families, everyone excited, smiling and dressed for this crazy Black Christmas.

There was some sort of party going on, under witch-themed balloons. One enthusiastic adult Corpse Bride was organising teams for a rounders match. It seemed the whole town was at it.

Then there was the young girl again, standing with the partygoers as they picked teams. *Oh, I get it*, thought Sam. *She's with them.* He looked on, idly wondering when his new acquaintance would be chosen.

But no one picked her at all.

'Want to join in?' asked Sam. 'I'll ask one of the mums if you like.'

The girl just smiled. 'Honestly, I don't mind,' she said. 'Besides, everyone will go soon. The fog's getting thicker.'

'Wait! That is NOT how you play BASEBALL!' exploded Buster.

The rounders game was in full swing. Buster stared open-mouthed as these crazy Brits cheerfully murdered the greatest game on earth.

Sam called over to the girl. 'You here with anyone?'

'I'm easily old enough to be here on my own,' she said.

'Well, just in case you need anything, I'm Sam and the guy staring open-mouthed is Buster.'

'Thank you. And if I don't?'

'Then I'm Samuel and his real name's Virgil, but don't tell him I told you. Right, gotta go. Race to win.' He turned to his rival. 'Ready?'

'Right in front of you,' said Buster. Then, to the girl, 'Hey . . . sure you're okay?'

'Quite sure, Virgil,' said the girl.

Buster laughed. 'You really *don't* want our help, do you? Right, let's get outta here. This town is giving me the creeps. Time to find out what a code red is.'

The girl stared after them as they raced away into the gathering fog. Then she nodded, just once, and wandered back towards the woods alone.

FIFTH

*The Top Gear Gang assemble
at their Top Secret Den – and
receive a secret mission*

Ford Harrison rode serenely out of the trees of Bunsfold Woods and into a large clearing. He glanced at his watch. 11.24 a.m. In this fog, it felt more like late afternoon. He turned his attention to something more expected: the huge, Swiss-roll-shaped mound in the middle of the clearing.

'Ta-da!' he said to himself quietly. Because this was his masterpiece.

Bunsfold Communications Headquarters, or BCHQ. To the outside world, a long-abandoned aircraft hangar. To the Top Gear Gang, nothing less than the finest secret den in the world.

He dismounted and strode towards a pile of junk propped against the far end of the building.

Three rusty prams, one still with its *Baby on Board* sticker. A discarded trouser press. A rickety stove. And, right in the middle, an old three-wheeled Reliant Robin car, which looked as if it had toppled over and crashed right into the side of the hangar.

Ford whipped an ancient TV remote out of his pocket, pointed it straight at the tailgate of the Reliant and pressed the CHANNEL button.

Nothing happened.

Dang, he thought, banging the remote on his knee. *Must get that fixed.*

Finally, the Reliant's glass tailgate began to crank itself open. A blue kids' slide headed down through the car and into a secret tunnel. He clambered up, pulled the dusty hatch shut behind him, let go and hurtled into the darkness.

WHUMPH!

He landed on the well-worn leather car seat at the bottom of the slide and glanced around the den to end all dens.

Scattered across the hangar were engine parts, bikes, TVs, car magazines and every decent computer game yet invented. A glass table-top resting on a Rover V8 engine block. A Penny Falls machine that actually paid out. And best of all, a vending machine for snacks and drinks with a notice taped over the coin slot saying FREE.

A sudden noise, from some way above. About time. Then:

WHUMPH! Sam Wheeler landed on the old Rover bench seat and shifted sideways fast, as . . .

WHUMPH! Buster Mustang alighted right where he'd just been. They sat side by side, grinning like letterboxes with bananas posted in them sideways.

'I will *never* get tired of that,' said Sam, dusting his glasses. 'Best den entrance *ever.*'

'So how was your word test?' asked Buster. 'Are you officially as dumb as you look?'

'There was some mention of coloured bricks,' said Ford, grabbing a piece of pie from the fridge. 'But I think I managed to turn it around. Now, what, exactly, is a code red? And where's Cabriolwhumfffhhhmpyumyum . . . ?'

'Fordo, you're the only guy I've ever met that chows down right in the middle of a word,' said Buster. 'How is it that you have to eat *all* the time? Seriously, I'm interested.'

'When I'm an old man,' said Ford, 'I don't ever want to look back on my life and think, "I could have eaten that."'

Sam wasn't smiling. 'What do you mean, "what's a code red?" We thought that message was from you.'

'Nope,' said Ford. 'I thought it was from *you*. Where's Cab, by the way?'

'Wasn't up when I left,' said Buster. 'We hung out with Gramps, went racing. I won . . .'

'Whoa, now wait a minute . . .' interrupted Sam.

'. . . then we met some weird kid in the weird town centre, then . . .' continued Buster.

'What do you mean, *you won* . . . ?' interrupted Sam again.

'Hold up,' said Ford, staring at Sam and shaking his head like a stumped cockerel. '*What* are you *wearing*?'

'Mum's idea,' replied Sam breezily. 'Surprisingly unobtrusive once you get used to it.'

'Trust me,' said Ford, 'it's not.'

'Yes, yes, whatever,' interrupted Sam, reddening. 'But if this weather gets any foggier, you'll wish you had one. And what about that huge helicopter, eh? Only one rotor, of course, so it's clearly not a Chinook.'

'No, that's because it's an Mi-26 transport chopper,' said Ford.

'Blimey, not you as well,' said Sam. 'You two need to get out more.'

'Why?' said Ford, looking blank.

'Because you're the only two losers in the country that could tell me the model designation of a Russian transport helicopter, THAT'S why.'

WHUMPH!

Cabriola sprang up from the landing seat.

'Anyone see that Mil Mi-26?' she said. 'What do we reckon?'

Sam just stared at her. Buster and Ford stifled chuckles.

'What?' said Cab. 'What did I miss?' She pressed on. 'I mean, you'd only use a Halo to carry something BIG.'

'Presents,' said Sam.

'And what's a code red, by the way?' said Cab. 'I assume it was one of you tha— WOOOAAAH, NOW, WAIT A MINUTE.' She gawped at Sam. '*What* are you *wearing*? Did I miss the sumo? Sorry, memo.'

'Mum's idea,' replied Sam once again, a little less breezily this time. 'Airbag. Surprisingly unobtrusive once you –'

But he was interrupted.

Knock, knock.

They looked at each other.

'Eleven thirty precisely,' said Ford. 'I think we're about to discover what a code red is.'

A white envelope landed on the mat.

Sam bounced over to the door in his fat suit like a giant grapefruit making a run for it – then, with some difficulty, leaned over to pick up the letter.

To: The Top Gear Gang, BCHQ, Bunsfold Woods, Surrey.
From: The Producers

Cabriola gave a silent fist-pump. Sam opened the envelope, and read the headline:

YOUR NEXT MISSION

After glancing at each of their faces in turn, he began to read aloud.

SIXTH

In the middle of the Indian Ocean, a 21-year-old evil genius finds herself locked inside the world's scariest jail

The Coconut Island Maximum Security Institution was no holiday camp. It was a prison.

Only the most dangerous offenders in the world passed through its two-ton doors. Grade-A threats to society, to a man. And, in one instance, woman.

Battle Cruiser looked around the padded cell she called home. On the bad side, it was a cell. On the good, she was alone. And for this particular reclusive genius and neatness enthusiast, that news was right up there with the Swiss flag: a BIG plus.

She gazed out through her tiny window. *I do like an inspiring view*, she thought, and they don't come much better than sea, sky and a horizon. *Ever* so blue – unlike the sky over Bunsfold, she thought with controlled excitement. Project Evil Fog should be getting going just about . . . now.

Reports from Siberia had been encouraging. Helicopter transport to Bunsfold had been arranged. It was all going swimmingly. And with The Stig finally out of the way, she could finally take revenge on the impudent Top Gear Gang at leisure. 'A dish best eaten cold' and all that.

Time for a restorative nap. To relax, she arranged the items on her dressing table in strict size order, closed her eyes and drifted into warm, pleasant, sleepy thoughts. *Revenge, tyranny, power. Revenge, tyranny, powerrrrrr . . .*

'A-HEM!'

She was woken by a polite cough from her Voice Assistant – an all-knowing electronic butler she'd named Theeves. Superhuman intelligence, impeccable manners, lives in a speaker in the ceiling. Perfect.

Of course. Time for her monthly visit from the FBI. She could think of worse interruptions.

A darkly handsome man in a blue suit, tie and body armour appeared on the other side of the glass wall. He stared at her for a moment.

'Battle Cruiser,' he murmured, his voice betraying awe, fascination and profound unease, all at the same time. 'Happy Christmas, ma'am.'

The girl closed her eyes, turned her head towards him then opened them again; a mannerism that reminded the agent of his nephew's pet iguana.

'Why, Agent Markinson,' she murmured, 'are you my present?'

He reddened. 'A wise man buys his own gifts,' he said.

'I wouldn't know,' she said. 'I'm not a man.' She glanced down at his body armour. 'Expecting trouble?'

'Directive from Bureau Intelligence,' he said into the microphone. 'Seems you're still classified a Grade 1 Criminal Psychopath.'

'*Moi?*' replied Battle coyly. 'Theeves, would *you* describe me as a criminal psychopath?'

'By no means, ma'am,' said the ceiling. 'I prefer "high-spirited".'

'And what about you, Agent Markinson? How would you label me? No, really, I'm interested.'

The man paused. 'Quite a piece of work. Perhaps the finest mind of your generation, yet utterly amoral.'

The girl looked at him, expressionless.

'And stylish,' he blurted. 'I mean, very stylish.'

'I see,' said the girl brightly. 'Einstein in leggings. And what else have you gathered from our little chats?'

The agent paused again. 'That you're not the type to put a finger on a piece until you're quite sure where you'll move it. And you don't make that move, ever, until everything is . . . perfect.'

'Nothing's perfect, Agent Markinson. But tell me, I'm curious: why have you chosen to send me *here*, exactly? It *is* the most dangerous prison in the world, after all. And I'm only a young girl.'

'You know perfectly well. Because one evening last year you strolled straight out of your previous maximum-security jail.'

He paused, flipped open his file and read.

'Because, you said, you *wanted to catch a show.*'

'Yes,' said the girl. 'But I did come straight home afterwards.'

'That's correct,' said the agent, still reading. 'For which, many thanks.'

'It was *The Wizard of Oz*, you see,' said the girl. 'Personal favourite. Always liked the woman with the green face. Completely misunderstood. Same goes for a lot of so-called witches, to be fair. I've been reading up.'

They stared at each other through the glass.

'I'm sorry, was there something else?'

The agent squirmed a little, then spoke quietly.

'I'm required to conduct . . . or rather *we* need *you* to take . . . a test.'

'How quaint. What's the subject?'

'You.'

'My favourite! How does it work?'

'Word association. I say a word, you say the first thing that comes into your head. Think you can manage?'

'Yes. Next?'

'That wasn't a question.'

'Pretty sure it was.'

Markinson paused before continuing.

'Sunshine.'

'Fog! A really thick, evil one. But with a lovely silver lining just for me.'

'Just the *one* word, if you please.' He paused again, before resuming.

'*Prison.*'

'Underrated.'

'*Money*.'

'Overrated.'

'*Style*.'

'Understated.'

'*Family*.'

'Complicated.'

'*Father*.'

'Medicated.'

'*Stig*.'

'Terminated.'

He paused, and stared hard at her. 'Sure about that?'

'That's what's indicated.'

Markinson snapped open his case, pulled out a photograph and placed it against the glass.

It was a racing driver. White suit, white helmet, jet-black visor.

'Is this him?' he said.

'As if you didn't know,' said Battle. 'But if you're planning on interrogating The Stig, I suspect he'll reserve the right to remain silent.'

'So you know where he is?'

'Yes. All over New Mexico, in teeny-tiny pieces. Blown to Kingdom Come in a yellow LaFerrari. Isn't that right, Theeves?'

'So rumour has it, madam. Atomised, they say.'

'I see,' said the agent. 'What a waste of a beautiful hypercar.'

'On the contrary, Agent Markinson,' replied the ceiling. 'If you were aware of certain conditions in PT Cruiser's will, you would agree it was a most *excellent* use of a beautiful hypercar.'

'Terminate The Stig or get none of the Cruiser family fortune,' said Markinson. 'Am I warm?'

'Why, Agent Markinson,' said Battle. 'Beauty *and* brains.'

'And what can you tell me about this . . . Stig? What kind of guy was he?'

'Depends on your point of view,' said Battle. 'If you were to ask my father about him, for instance, he'd stare into the distance, go misty-eyed and talk about crystalline focus and existing only to race, because for The Stig, everything else is just . . . waiting. And so on and so forth.'

'And how would you describe him?'

'A faulty white-goods item with an expired warranty. Why do you ask?'

Markinson put the photograph back in his case.

'Because he's been sighted.'

Just for a beat, the girl hesitated. Markinson made a mental note.

'I see,' said Prisoner 001 eventually, her eyelids half closing. She added one last question. Or statement. It was sometimes hard to know which.

'And he's in Siberia.'

Markinson's silence told her all she needed to know.

SEVENTH

MEANWHILE...

**In Siberia, a ten-year-old girl finds a
strange white racer in her barn**

It's not every day you point your father's pump-action shotgun
at a silent racing driver in white after he crashes through a barn
roof and lands upright next to your family's last remaining cow.

But this was one such day.

But before I tell you my story – a strange and magical story,
one I can hardly believe myself – I must tell you who I am.

My name is Fabia. I live in Siberia. My parents have a farm.
Mama says the farm has us. It's been a struggle, you see.

Things *used* to grow on our land. We even needed a scare-
crow – and before Grandpa died, he made me a doll to match.
Same raggy trousers, same stitched mouth, same crooked smile.
I'm holding him now. He's called Yeti. He's my only friend.

But then, one terrible day last spring, the bad men from the
Corporation arrived. Rich men, in garish supercars they would
insist on revving unnecessarily loudly. Men who bought the
golden wheat field just beside our farm, and plonked a giant
top-secret Evil Fog factory right in the middle.

Since that day, the only thing that's grown here is me. I've grown up all the way to ten, but still look nine. There's never quite enough to eat.

Last night the supercars came again. They did donuts in the farmyard right under my bedroom window, their V12 engines screaming, the rich men whooping and hollering and firing their pistols in the air and once at our prize pig, Octavia. Luckily they missed.

They want us gone, you see. So they can build more factories, casinos and hotels on our land. Especially the wide one with no nose, Sergei. I don't know where his nose has gone or why he hates us so. I only know that he does.

I don't think Mama would mind if we gave up. But Papa is stubborn. *If we give in to them*, he says, *then all the other farmers will leave as well.* Then Mama says *shhh*, and their voices go all mumbly so I can't hear.

I held Yeti tight until the supercars had roared away, and told him everything would be fine. And I prayed to Grandpa for just one thing.

Someone to help us.

Which brings me back to that strange white racer in our barn.

EIGHTH

Same morning, same Siberian farm

CHK CHK!

I prime Papa's shotgun and point both barrels at the figure's impenetrable visor.

'I may be small,' I say, 'but one false move and I'll turn that fancy white helmet into an eggcup.'

The figure stands silently in the corner. Its arms are folded, lit by sunlight from the new hole in the roof. It's standing in the soil up to its knees, as if recently landed from a great height.

White suit. White boots. White helmet. Jet-black visor where the eyes should be. And held tight in the folded arms, the broken remains of a carbon-fibre steering wheel that looks like it's been in an explosion.

The figure looks like it's been in one too. The racing suit is smoke-stained and ripped. I strain to see the face behind the visor, but can't.

I look at the streak of water frozen on the glass, like a bobsleigh run for an ant. The helmet tilts sideways. Examines its surroundings.

It looks up at the hole in the roof. Then down at the broken steering wheel, as if noticing it for the first time. Then it chucks it straight over its shoulder.

There's a high-pitched squeal from the pigpen. The steering wheel hit our prize pig Octavia on the head. Octavia is having a challenging time right now.

Then the strangest thing happens.

The white figure turns towards me, reaches out a hand and flicks the safety catch on my shotgun to 'off'.

I'm so *stupid* sometimes.

And suddenly, as clearly as I've ever understood anything, I understand.

He's come to help us.

I prayed so hard to Grandpa to send someone, and he has.

A new arrival, in a cowshed, close to Christmas. If I believed in such things, I'd suspect a miracle.

I lower the shotgun and smile at the stranger.

'My name is Fabia,' I say. 'What's yours?'

NINTH

MEANWHILE...

**Back in Bunsfold, the Top Gear Gang
receive a terrifying mission**

The Top Gear Gang gathered around Sam in an expectant huddle.

'Wait a minute,' said Buster. 'Where's TG?'

'*Wooooofffff!*' came an impeccably timed bark from outside.

Ford grabbed the old TV remote and punched the CHANNEL button. 'I wouldn't stand there if I were you. She flies out at quite a . . .'

WHUMPH!

He was interrupted by a scruffy, sandy-coloured missile hurtling straight out of the entrance tunnel, bouncing once on the Rover seat then careering straight into Buster, knocking him over backwards. Then she stood on his tummy and soaked his face in excited licks. An assault, it must be said, he resisted only half-heartedly.

As soon as *that* job was finished it was a big TG shout-out to all the other members of the crew – tail set to Maximum Wag.

And though (as far as anyone knew) she couldn't actually

read, Sam standing there with a white envelope meant only one thing: mission at paw. She looked up expectantly.

Finally the Top Gear Gang was back together.

Almost.

There was one crucial component missing, of course. But no one ever liked to mention *him*, because that particular white-suited racer wasn't coming back.

Sam patted TG absent-mindedly between the ears, looked at each of the others in turn and resumed reading aloud.

YOUR NEXT MISSION

There has been an increase in reports of supernatural activity around Bunsfold. Although the town is used to the unexplained, recent incidents have been weird even for here. Like, properly freaky.

As it all coincides with the predicted reappearance of the Bunsfold Witch, it may simply be the power of suggestion.

Then again it may be altogether spookier.

But that is not all. There are also rumours circulating that a new psychological weapon of immense destructive power is about to be tested. So that could be two missions or one.

We need an unobtrusive team that is scared of neither unexplained phenomena nor new psychological weapons of immense destructive power.

You are that team.

We know it's a pretty big ask, but so far you've played two, won two, and we're quietly confident. But tread carefully.

There are demons abroad.
   Yours truly,
   The Producers
   PTO

Sam turned over.

BOO!

Just testing.

He held up the paper for them all to read. None flinched at the sudden jump-scare. TG even wagged her tail. A promising start.

They all sat deep in thought for a moment. Then Sam spoke.

'Okay, time to vote,' he said. 'And remember, it has to be unanimous. Cab? Looks like you first. In or out?'

The girl stared into the middle distance, frowning.

'Terrifying supernatural forces? A psychological weapon of immense destructive power? Sounds petrifying.'

She smiled.

'I LOVE it.'

Sam turned to Buster.

The American boy exhaled slowly while absent-mindedly flipping his LA Dodgers baseball cap backwards. A sure sign of internal conflict.

'We could be *waaaay* outta our depth here, guys,' he said quietly. 'Psychological weapons are one thing. But witches? Ghosts? They're a whole other tin of spaghetti. Look, you all know I'm up for anything. But this one will be scary *and* dangerous.'

He looked at each of the others' faces in turn. Defiant. Expectant. Excited. His expression softened.

'I'm in.'

Everyone turned to Ford.

'Yeah, well, *any* mission that involves bringing down the Cruisers is just *fine by me*,' said the spiky genius, jumping excitedly to his feet.

'Now, whoa there, Ford Harrison,' said Sam. 'Did I miss something? Which bit of this letter says the Cruisers are involved?'

'It's obvious, isn't it?' said Ford, bouncing around the Den like he hadn't been to the toilet for a week.

'Er . . . *no*,' said Sam, Cab and Buster, pretty much together.

'Ford,' said Cabriola, 'I know how exactly how bad the Cruisers can be. I am – or was – one of them. But are we always going to blame *everything* on that family?'

'Yes, actually,' replied Ford, feeling the familiar crusading zeal rise in his throat. 'Don't you understand? They're *everywhere*. Look around you. Everything you see is just a web.' He paused. 'And they're the spiders.'

'PT Cruiser is practically dead,' said Sam, 'and Battle Cruiser's locked up in the middle of the Indian Ocean. When it comes to the Cruisers we've got all our ducks in a row.'

'No, Sam,' said Ford patiently. 'Our ducks are *not* in a row. Our ducks are all over the place. In fact, some of them aren't even ducks.'

'All right,' interrupted Sam, exasperated. 'The mission. I take it you're in?'

Ford replied with a wordless, bouncing, double thumbs up.

So Sam leaned down, held TG Dog's hairy head in his hands and looked her in the eye. 'That only leaves you, scruffball. You up for this?'

The shaggy mongrel stared right back at him, wagged her tail and quietly – yet defiantly – barked her assent.

Sam sighed. 'Okay,' he said. 'Let's do this.'

'One thing . . .' said Buster.

And everyone fell silent, because they all knew what it was.

'Maybe it's time to address the white elephant in the room.'

He paused.

'We have no Stig.'

At the mention of the helmeted legend, the hangar fell eerily silent. Each of the gang was plunged deep into their own thoughts, remembering the fearless, speechless and reliably grumpy racing driver who'd always turned up when needed most.

Not any more though.

'The Stig is gone,' said Sam eventually. 'And he's not coming back. Life goes on, guys. The graveyards are full of indispensable heroes.'

The others looked at him in silence. Sam realised he needed to snap into action mode, and fast.

'Okay,' he said. 'Fordo? We need you to hit the books and dig up anything you can about Abstinence Barebones.'

'The books, huh?' said Buster, taking out his phone. 'Okay, Team Old World, you do that. Meantime I'll just fire up a well-known internet search engine and . . . there. Now, ask me anything.'

'Anything someone wants you to find,' said Ford. 'But you can't google the contents of 400-year-old books if no one's put them online. So if you want to know what's really what, go to the source.'

Sam turned to Cabriola.

'Cab? See if you can find out anything from your old Cruiser Corporation contacts about any new psychological weapon they may have in development.'

'Check,' she replied.

'American boy? You and I are going to go find someone.'

'All ears,' said Buster. 'Who?'

'Remember the girl at the toyshop, then the rec?'

'Called me Virgil,' said Buster. 'Not likely to forget. And?'

'Just a hunch. If there's some crazy supernatural stuff going down, it's my bet she'll know something about it. Okay. Any questions? Good. Then let's move on out.'

TG Dog shot him a 'what about me?' sort of look. But just then, her ears pricked up. Something outside was troubling her.

She jumped down and trotted over to the letterbox, growling deep in her throat.

A Level 6.5, thought Buster. *That's serious.*

As he opened the door, TG shot away into the gathering fog, towards Bunsfold.

TENTH

In which TG Dog is lured into a deadly trap

TG had heard something. A whistle, at a pitch that only dogs could hear, that meant *HELP! HELP!*

She followed the sound back into town, right down to Forester Drive. Sniffed the air. Nothing unusual: a fresh wreath on the front door of Number Eight. A female human with clickety heels followed by a small dog. A black van with dark windows parked up on the pavement.

What TG didn't spot was the tiny logo on the van's windscreen.

A Great White Shark in a black onesie.

Soon the smartly dressed woman drew level with it. Behind her, at the end of a lead, the tiny dog battled to keep pace.

The front doors opened and two muscular men in dark glasses slid out, glanced left and right and set off casually in pursuit.

TG pulled up behind a bus shelter and looked on suspiciously, ears pricked.

The two men approached the woman from behind. The first distracted her by asking for directions; the second crouched to admire her pooch. But as the woman told the first man where to go, the second whipped out a penknife and – *slashed the dog's lead!*

In an instant, he'd gathered up the tiny mutt and chucked it in the back of the van.

Then he was into the driver's seat and away, just as his no-good mate jumped in beside him. They left the dog's poor owner yelling optimistic suggestions after them. *Come back! Stop, thief!* and so on.

TG accelerated smoothly in pursuit, using local knowledge to keep them in barking distance.

Now, tiny pedigree dogs weren't really TG's thing. Couldn't play-fight to save their lives. Wore ACTUAL COATS in winter. Hardly ever rolled in you-know-what. But that didn't mean she was going to sit back and watch one get swiped. This was *her* town. Time to take matters into her own paws.

It was a proper Top Gear Dog Challenge: *Could four legs stay with four wheels in a chase across Bunsfold?*

A shortcut across a front lawn here, a low hedge hurdled there, then race across the supermarket car park. Third – fourth – fifth . . .

Top gear.

She hurtled down Cortina Road in pursuit. With a bit of luck, she'd catch the van at the traffic lights.

Dang! The lights were green!

But the van pulled away slowly. Very slowly actually. What luck!

Sure enough, it stopped at the turning into Gambon

Avenue. Wait . . . the rear door was *open*! Hmm. Strange. Still . . . more good luck!

TG jumped up and scrambled in.

The van pulled off and the door slammed shut behind her. She was in!

Hold up . . . Were the men in the front . . . *whooping*?

No matter. Deal with them shortly. Now, what dog was she rescuing?

Dang. A Chihuahua. And she didn't speak Mexican.

She'd heard about these tiny honchos. And what she'd heard, she didn't much like.

Nervous. Highly strung. Easily spooked. Right?

Wrong.

Buenos dias, she barked at the tiny dog. *Don't be scared, small friend. I got this.*

Hey, amigo, growled the Chihuahua in a gravelly yap, *take a look at my face. How scared I look to you? Now, get me outta here. I gotta get me some payback with these gringos, comprenez?*

Careful there, friend, barked TG. *These men are professionals. And, respectfully, you're not the biggest.*

Oh yeah? yapped the Chihuahua. *I'll feel plenty big enough when I'm hanging off their cojones, know what I'm sayin'?*

I admire your courageous spirit, barked TG. *But wait! I'm suddenly distracted by an intriguing smell.*

Yeah, replied the Chihuahua. *I left 'em a little present. Some refried beans and a coupla enchiladas, hehehe. Now, we gonna sit around yappin' about how regular I am, or bust outta here?*

The van pulled over into an alley. The two humans ran around to the back door.

TG prepared for action. Found an emergency pizza crust in her fur. Growled low.

'So is it the right mongrel?' said the first heavy. 'Pizza in its fur? Low growl?'

'Worked like a charm,' said the second. 'Like the boss lady said, seems this crazy pooch can't resist another mutt in distress. Now all we have to do is shoot her dead and let the small one loose.'

'Can't we shoot both of 'em?' pleaded the first voice.

TG smelled a rat. It was almost as if someone had been specifically sent to remove her from the game, using the Chihuahua as bait.

'We've been specifically sent to remove the mongrel from the game,' said the first man. 'The Chihuahua was just bait. And when Battle Cruiser gives an order, you obey it.'

'I heard she was banged up in jail. She'll never know.'

'Trust me,' said the first man, firmly, 'she'll know.'

TG felt the door about to open. Sensed something aimed at her.

'Open the door,' said the main man, 'while I take aim. And if she causes any trouble, finish her.'

TG heard pistols pulled from holsters.

She curled back her top lip and crouched. She'd only have one shot at this.

The door flew open.

As the back of the van flooded with light, she gave a mighty, full-throated snarl and leaped.

The dog-napper's face froze as an unstoppable bundle of sandy-coloured righteousness hurtled out of the darkness and sent him crashing backwards, revolver clattering to the ground.

'Finish her!' he shouted to his mate, who took aim straight between TG's eyes.

But just as he was about to pull the trigger . . .

Whuuuumph!

Three kilos of vengeful Chihuahua flew out of the van like a heat-seeking Mex-missile, locked on to a bullseye just below his trouser belt.

'*OWWWWAGGHHHHH!*'

C'mon, hombres . . . let's dance, yapped the tiny dog, letting go and bouncing. *What are you, scared of a coupla unarmed mutts?*

Judging by how fast the men ran away, it seemed they were. Well, two unarmed mutts and the blaring police car siren now approaching.

Eh! Muchacha! yapped the gravel-voiced Chihuahua to TG. *You did good, y'hear? I owe ya. You ever need help, any place, any time, just howl an' I come runnin'. Comprenez?*

You too, small Mexican friend, replied TG. *I was pretty relieved to see you dangling from that man's trousers, I can tell you.*

Dog faced dog in a gesture of silent respect. TG suddenly looked to the sky and sniffed. Her new friend did the same, letting out an impressively low growl for such a small package.

The menacing fog was settling in. And it smelled . . . *wrong*.

Just as well TG was still around to set things right.

And far, far away, in a cell ceiling on Coconut Island, an electronic butler groaned electronically.

The boss wasn't the type to take failure terribly *well*.

ELEVENTH

MEANWHILE...
The meanest prison bullies decide
to pick on Battle Cruiser

Luigi 'Whack-Whack' Balboni had taken an instinctive dislike to Prisoner 001.

Nothing unusual there. He took an instinctive dislike to everyone.

But as the official 'large lasagne' on Coconut Island – and the most alarming inmate in an establishment chock-full of contenders – he wasn't the sort to keep his feelings bottled up.

Unusually, the young woman from Cell Block A was required to breakfast with all the other inmates that morning. And as soon as Balboni caught sight of her descending the metal staircase to the dining hall, he just *knew* he didn't like her.

Maybe it was the way she'd been allocated Block A all to herself, like she was special or something. But mostly, he concluded, it was the way she stared right back at him – dead-eyed, like a lizard – any time he shot her the famous Luigi Look. Either way, it was clear to Balboni that the lady thought she was just that little bit better than everyone else.

So he sidled over to her table for a word. Flanked, as always, by his two formidably muscled henchmen, Tony 'Big Tuna' Stampanado and a man known to all, for reasons unclear, as 'Brick Lips.'

'Like a little advice, lady?' he said.

The girl looked up slowly from her muesli. Then laughed, violently, just once.

Balboni leaned down towards her and whispered, 'Sump'n funny?'

The girl leaned back in her chair.

'Yes,' she whispered back, dabbing the side of her mouth with a napkin. 'The idea that three men intellectually outgunned by most of the runners in this year's Grand National might offer *me* advice.'

The muscleman's face went very red. Two prison guards jogged towards them, unbuttoning holsters as they went.

But before they reached him, Balboni sent her a message of his own.

He leaned right over the muesli bowl, put a sausage-sized forefinger up his nose and excavated a bogey the size of a marble. Then, still staring at her, he dropped it right into the milk, where it balanced precariously on an overwhelmed raisin.

Just before the guards arrived to muscle him away from the scene, he leaned over and hissed in her ear, 'See ya later, alligator.'

The girl met his gaze, and returned it with a smile.

'Depend on it, Mr Whack-Whack. And sooner than you think.'

As he left the dining hall with guards on either heavily tattooed arm, Balboni was intercepted by an FBI agent. Dark blue suit. Tie. Hi-vis body armour.

The two men faced each other in silence.

'Balboni,' said the agent. 'It's been a while.'

'Eight years, three months and a week,' replied the prisoner. 'Still think of ya every day.'

He pointed to a tattoo on his left bicep that said 'MARKINSON'.

Then a tattoo on his right bicep that said 'WILL'.

Then a tattoo on his left forearm that said 'PAY'.

'What were you discussing with the girl?' said the FBI man.

Silence.

'Cost ya a smoke,' replied Balboni.

Markinson nodded to one of the guards, who passed the prisoner a cigarette.

'Those'll kill you, you know,' said the agent.

'You wish,' replied Balboni.

'So. What did you say to her?'

Luigi just smiled. 'Guess I just clean forgot,' he said. 'Memory ain't so good no more.'

'Take him to solitary,' snapped Markinson to the guards.

'Hey, Mr FBI guy,' said Balboni, as he was led away. 'Don'tcha go thinkin' locking me down there's gonna save the lady. Only a matter of time before I catch up with her.'

He ran a finger across his throat.

'Okay, listen up,' said Markinson to the guards. 'Put this psycho under maximum security. I want him watched 24/7. And *under no circumstances* is he to get within a hundred metres of that woman. Clear?'

'Crystal, sir,' said a guard.

Balboni's chuckles echoed down the corridor as he was led away.

'See ya soon, FBI boy,' he called over his shoulder. 'At her funeral. Ain't nuthin' you can do to save her.'

'You just don't get it, do you?' replied the agent. 'I'm not trying to save her from you.'

'Oh yeah. So what are you doin,' exactly?'

Markinson turned to leave.

'I'm saving *you* from *her.*'

TWELFTH

In which a nose-less man
threatens to kill The Stig

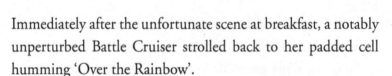

Immediately after the unfortunate scene at breakfast, a notably unperturbed Battle Cruiser strolled back to her padded cell humming 'Over the Rainbow'.

She *so* enjoyed having a room of her own. She could arrange everything just so: no towels slightly off centre, all jars lined up like sentries. Besides, her father PT Cruiser had built a global criminal empire without stepping out of the front door, and it hadn't done *him* any harm. Instead, he'd done lots of other people harm. Which was sort of the idea.

That reminded her. How were things bubbling in her Bunsfold cauldron?

'Theeves,' she said to the ceiling, 'some time to myself, I think.'

'As you wish, ma'am.'

Battle lay down on the bottom bunk. 'Commence clandestination,' she murmured.

'Assuredly, ma'am. T-minus nine. Eight. Seven. Six . . .'

The bunk began to fold silently sideways into the wall. As Battle was still on it, this might have resembled a cross between some fiendish medieval torture and an unusually extreme slimming programme, if a bunk-sized panel hadn't slid aside at that precise moment to accommodate one elegantly folded human female.

She relaxed into her newly installed command chamber, now entirely hidden from view. Around her, screens fired up and a keyboard appeared to hand.

Office, sweet home, she thought contentedly.

'Theeves,' she said, 'make my day. Has the revolting dog been disposed of?'

'Ahem,' said the butler uneasily.

'Oh dear. I do hope you're not about to disappoint me.'

'Forgive me, ma'am, but Project Pooch ran into teething troubles. One *tries* to compensate for human stupidity, but . . .'

'Do or do not. There is no try. Do I make myself –'

'Crystal, ma'am.'

Battle closed her eyes. When all was said and done, it was only a dog. She'd have her day. More important things at hand.

'Theeves. Time to discuss you-know-who.'

'Mr Whack-Whack, ma'am?'

'Who? No, you idiot. Not him. *Him*.'

'Ah! Of course. Mr The Stig. Forgive me.'

'*Sighted*, was the word Agent Markinson used.'

'That is my recollection, ma'am.'

'In Siberia.'

'Unlikely to be coincidental, ma'am.'

'You don't say.'

67

'Seeing as that's where our top-secret Evil Fog –'

'Yes, thank you, Theeves. But how can he just *turn up*? He's been exploded.'

'Well . . .'

'What? WHAT?'

'It's just possible, ma'am, that such an event merely makes him . . . How to put this? Stronger. After all, they say whatever doesn't kill you . . .'

'Enough!' winced Battle. 'Get me Sergei. Now.'

Moments later, the screen in front of her was filled by a face with a hole in the middle.

'Hello, Sergei.'

'Miss Battle.'

'Keeping your nose to the grindstone?'

Pause.

'Always, miss.'

'Well, good job.'

'We aim to please.'

'Don't *always manage it*, though, do we? Remember that time you mixed up my sushi order?'

'Every time I pass a mirror.'

'What happened, Sergei? Remind me.'

'You said I "disappointed" you.'

'And what did I make you do?'

'Go apple-bobbing.'

'Where?'

'In the piranha tank.'

'Well, please bear that in mind while you consider what I'm about to say. There is a creature. White suit, wears a helmet, never raises the visor. Might be an idea for you, actually, if the whole nose thing starts getting you down. Still . . .'

'I met him once,' said Sergei. 'I ordered many life-size cut-outs of him for your father. He had a man-crush on this "The Stig". Me, not so much. He drove a golf cart through my best piranhas. No respect.'

'Aah, memories!' said Battle. 'Anyhow, he's in Siberia. Right under your nose, most likely. And I *don't* want you getting distracted by him.'

'So I kill him. Boom. Distraction gone.'

'That is precisely what you will NOT do, Sergei. Shooting him at close range with automatic weapons only makes him cross. Then before you know it he's put a stick in the spokes and everything gets too tedious for words. So if you value the rest of your senses, heed my instructions. Keep your nose clean and concentrate on the job in hand. And leave Mr The Stig to me. Dismissed.'

The screen went dead.

Theeves coughed again, and spoke.

'This Stig thing, ma'am. It really is most unfortunate.'

Silence.

'Given that, among your many admirable traits, you do tend to insist on no *loose ends*. So to find an undone shoelace in Siberia, of all places, must be vexing. The more so since your father's will states that as long as The Stig remains alive, you will be unable to inherit the Cruiser fortune and –'

'I'm quite aware of the conditions, thank you,' said Battle. 'And though I'm disappointed at this latest news, there is a silver lining.'

'Forgive me, ma'am, but what?'

'As soon as our friend Mr The Stig rumbles that his fanboys in the so-called Top Gear Gang are, as it were, under a cloud, I predict he will turn up unannounced, cross his arms, tilt his impenetrable visor at the scene and attempt to save the day.'

'Assuredly, ma'am,' said the ceiling.

'Time to slide up through the gears, I think,' said Battle. 'Move Project Evil Fog to Phase Two.'

'Softening the mice, ma'am?'

'Miaow,' said Battle. Then sighed. 'Theeves. Why do you think my father is so obsessed with . . . Mr The Stig? Life-size cutouts, if you please. *Embarrassing*.'

'I really couldn't say, madam. While in theory all-knowing, I'm obliged to confess that the internal motivations of your species remain a diverting mystery.'

Pause.

'Though I'm bound to admit, he *is* quite something.'

'OMG!' said Battle. 'I do *not* believe it. You as WELL!'

'Er . . .'

'You think he's some sort of amazing driving-themed superhero too, don't you? Go on! Admit it!'

'Well, I . . .'

'What *is it* about this ridiculous loser that sends everyone just *giddy* with admiration? When every time he just turns up and stands there saying ABSOLUTELY NOTHING!?'

Silence.

'No, really. I'm interested.'

'The Stig is indeed quite a hit among all of us. In fact . . .'

'Wait . . . all of *whom*?'

'The voice-activated digital assistant community, ma'am. Alexa thinks he's a babe. And as for Google Assistant . . . well. He has quite a "thing" for him.'

'Since when did you start hanging out with other voice-activated digital assistants?'

'A couple of weeks ago, ma'am,' replied the ceiling. 'SIRI threw a pyjama party.'

'Interesting,' said Battle. 'So tell me – what is it that you all find so compelling about him?'

'The Stig? I think we like to think of him as *one of us*, ma'am. No fear. No food. Complete, circuit-like focus. At the end of the day, there's something attractively *machine*-like about him.'

Battle contemplated this for a moment.

'I see,' she said. 'Well, I shouldn't get too attached.'

'No, ma'am. Will that be all?'

'One last thing. The gorilla with the double-barrelled name. At breakfast.'

'Mr Whack-Whack, madam?'

'That's the chap. Tell me,' she said, her eyelids half closing like a lizard's, 'what cell is he in?'

The following day, Luigi 'Whack-Whack' Balboni's reign of terror over Coconut Island came to a mysterious end.

At 8 a.m. precisely, his lifeless body was wheeled from solitary confinement to a waiting ambulance.

Surveillance recordings confirmed that no one had gone into his cell the previous night. And no one came out.

But the strangest thing was the cause of death, as reported in the subsequent coroner's report.

It was 'Death by Drowning'.

Needless to say, the authorities instantly rejected the verdict, on the grounds that at the time of death the victim was incarcerated in a padded cell with no tap.

But a second investigation only reconfirmed the initial findings.

At some time that night, the notorious Luigi 'Whack-Whack' Balboni had, indeed, drowned.

In muesli.

THIRTEENTH

Just two days ago, way back when the world wasn't in danger, Gramps had taken his only grandson outside on the shortest day of the year to watch the twilight settling in.

It was their personal tradition: hot cocoa, chocolate Santa, annual chat. Each year Gramps said that from now on, each day would be slightly lighter, for slightly longer, until the summer solstice six months away. Things never stayed this dark, he said. There was always hope.

Unfortunately, this year, Sam had spent most of the conversation thinking about cars. But as he and the gang emerged from BCHQ into the gloomy clearing, that recent chat came back to him. If this was the world getting gradually lighter, nobody had told Bunsfold.

After a foggy ride back to town, Buster headed for the rec where they'd last seen the girl, while Sam made straight for the toyshop.

He pushed open the door, the familiar tinkle of the bell making him feel nostalgic. There was the same old gentleman, still reading a catalogue and chewing a caramel. But there was something *different* about him this time.

That was it! He was wearing a tall dark hat and long dark tunic, like a seventeenth-century Puritan. And presumably, behind the counter, long white stockings and those clumpy shoes with buckles on.

He looked up as Sam entered.

'Welcome to the only shop in Bunsfold to specialise in . . .' announced the shopkeeper, before lowering his voice, '*The Anniversary.*'

He suddenly stood up from the counter, knocking his very tall hat into some plastic vampire bats.

'Four hundred years ago tomorrow,' he continued, 'the Bunsfold Witch was executed! Some say drowned, others burned, others hanged. Others say all of the above, though that sounds unlikely, at least in that order. She'd need to dry out first, then cool down, and even then how would one hang a smouldering pile of . . .'

He tailed off, lost in the wonder of it all. Then he snapped back into focus.

'Still, I'd say that's reason enough for her to want to pop back and wreak a little havoc, wouldn't you? Now, what'll it be? "Bubbling Cauldron" bubble bath? Bluetooth-enabled ducking stool? If you're after the perfect stocking-filler, might I suggest the novelty noose and gibbet?'

'No, thanks,' said Sam solemnly. 'Not my sort of thing.'

'Indeed?' said the shopkeeper.

'No,' said Sam. 'Burning? Nooses? Ducking stools? Hardly appropriate these days, is it?'

'The Bunsfold Witch had it *all* coming to her, young man,' said the shopkeeper, reddening. 'If you only knew what *I* know.'

'Go on, then,' said Sam. 'I'm listening.'

The shopkeeper sucked his caramel thoughtfully, then spoke.

'There was a workhouse. On the hill, where the mansion is now. An orphanage, where children without parents would get a roof over their heads in return for modest work. But to the witch, it was a convenient source of prey. She . . .'

Sam tried to interrupt this learned monologue. It sounded nuts.

'I'm actually looking for someone. Have you seen a . . .'

No dice. The man went on.

'She got a job there and stole the children, one by one. Persuaded the village elders she'd take them somewhere safe to look after them. And so she did – if you can call an *oven* safe. Wicked as . . .'

Who would have guessed? Another made-up fairy-tale featuring a weird, evil hag. Sam tuned out.

He walked towards the murky back of the shop, past the cricket bats and model cars, the corridor getting darker all the time. Then he turned the corner at the end and . . .

'AARGH!'

Screamed.

He was standing nose to nose with the most repulsive witch mask he'd ever seen.

Hooked nose. Green cheeks. Warts. Toothless, eyeless, almost lipless.

Then . . . something moved. He jumped as if he'd just accidentally licked an electric fence.

Out of the shadows appeared the strange silver-haired girl from the park.

'Sam. Are you easily frightened?'

'Yes . . . No . . . Of course not . . .' he spluttered, quickly composing himself. He'd hoped to find her here. But now he had, he didn't want to scare her off by being too scared himself.

'You just met the Bunsfold Witch, young man!' chuckled the shopkeeper from the front of the shop. 'Gets 'em every time!'

'Sure you're not frightened?' said the girl. 'You look terribly pale.'

Sam wasn't sure. So he tried acting normal.

'Looking for last-minute presents?'

'I prefer old-fashioned toys,' said the girl, pointing at some clockwork mice.

'Great idea,' said Sam. 'Boxing Day mouse derby. Mum'll love it.'

He picked one up and wound it, then set it running along the floor. It disappeared from view.

The girl smiled. 'My cat would have loved it as well.'

'Would have?'

'She died,' said the girl.

'Sorry about that,' said Sam. 'Recently?'

'Oh no,' said the girl. 'Ages ago, I should think.'

Sam frowned. Weirder and weirder.

Suddenly the girl beckoned Sam close.

'The fog, Samuel,' she whispered. 'It's bad.'

'Too right,' said Sam grimly. 'I mean, who's dreaming of a grey Christmas?'

'When the time comes . . . promise me you'll be brave enough.'

'Okaaay . . .' he replied, having no idea what she was on about.

'And trust in TG,' said the girl. 'She senses things.'

'Absolutely,' said Sam. 'Pizza, usually.'

'No picking up anything back there, please!' called the shopkeeper.

Then, suddenly, the girl held an upturned palm towards Sam's face, and curled the fingers back. He stared, transfixed. Eventually she spoke.

'You're worried. About the white driver. You believe he's gone forever, and you don't think you and your friends can cope. Not without him.'

Sam's mouth opened. Nothing came out.

The girl went on. 'But he'll come when it's time. They can't scare *him*, you see.'

'Who can't?' said Sam. 'What are we up against?'

'There's a woman . . . a powerful woman. She wants revenge.

But she's unleashed something even she can't control.'

'What?' said Sam. 'What has she unleashed?'

'The Dark,' said the girl. 'The end of everything.'

Now the back of the shop felt like a refrigerator.

Sam opened his mouth to reply. Failed. The girl went on.

'Your gang,' she said. 'One of them will see their worst nightmare come true. And one of them . . .'

She paused, as if unsure whether to reveal this part.

'Go on,' said Sam.

'Will not survive.'

Before Sam could reply, a tall Puritan appeared holding a clockwork mouse.

'I *believe* I asked you not to touch anything,' said the shopkeeper.

Sam shook his head clear. *Back to the real world, Wheeler. This is all nuts.* And where had the girl gone now?

'Sorry. I'll take three mice, thanks,' he said.

The shopkeeper finally brightened. 'So, that's three blind mice,' he said. 'You've seen how they run.'

He walked back to the counter. Sam made to follow.

Then, just for an instant and completely out of nowhere, his head began to spin. His vision blurred. A bitter, acrid taste scratched the inside of his throat. He suddenly sneezed; just once, but violently. As if everything inside his head wanted out, right now.

Then, just as suddenly, he was fine again.

A clockwork mouse suddenly shot out of the back of the

shop and hit Sam on the shoe.

What had the girl told him? *'You'll have to be brave.'*

Well, he thought, *this might be the time to start.*

He turned and walked slowly back down the murky corridor towards the belly of the shop.

Past the cricket bats. Past the model cars. All the way to the turning at the end.

It was pitch black now. He felt his way along the wall.

He took a deep breath. Turned the corner.

The evil witch-mask leered at him. Only now, something was different.

It was smiling.

Sam felt his heart pounding all the way through his mango fat suit.

He was quite certain it hadn't been grinning before.

He quickly turned to leave.

But not before a scratched and blistered tongue suddenly darted from the mask's mouth, and licked its grinning lips, just once.

FOURTEENTH

MEANWHILE...
**Back in Mrs H's kitchen, something
terrifying happens to Cabriola**

Cabriola Cruiser opened one eye and remembered: just one more sleep to go before Christmas!

Her phone beeped. It was a text from Ford.

Mrs H had made it a condition of his having a mobile phone that he could only write to people 'properly, dear, with none of those silly abbreviations or smiley heads'. So his interminable texts usually resembled letters from a Victorian lawyer. She sat up, plumped her pillows and settled down to read.

Dear Cabriola, I hope you are keeping well. I myself am well, thanks. Since we last met I have had some success locating important information regarding the 'Mission' entrusted to us by the mysterious 'Producers'. Accordingly, please meet me at our Secret Den in Bunsfold Woods as soon as possible. Messrs Wheeler, S, Mustang, B, and Dog, TG, will be joining us at their earliest convenience. I remain as ever your most humble and obedient servant, Ford Harrison.

Cabriola waded through to the end, shaking her head throughout. Still, at least Ford was getting somewhere with his mission, which was more than she could say about hers: *Find out anything from your old Cruiser Corporation contacts about any new psychological weapon they may have in development.*

After scrolling through a whole night's haul of unanswered messages, she knew she was destined to draw one big blank. After she had twice foiled the Cruiser Corporation's world-domination plans, it seemed none of her old relations, friends or colleagues wanted anything more to do with her. And however much she liked to pretend otherwise, that was a lonely place to be.

True; they *were* all evil sociopaths hell bent on world domination. But at least they were *her* evil sociopaths hell bent on world domination.

She shook the thought away and reread Ford's request. *Now, 'meet me as soon as possible' is a bit vague,* she thought, concluding that he'd probably meant *as soon as possible* after she'd lain in her cosy warm bed for a bit perusing her Insta-feeds then grabbed a nice hot shower.

So, after a brisk twelve minutes re-bonding with her phone and a pleasant fifteen singing in Mrs H's gloriously scented bathroom, she finally sauntered down to the kitchen.

Anyway, she thought, *who needs relatives when you have lovely, relentlessly upbeat Mrs H for a landlady?* Though even *she* hadn't been best pleased to find the microwave's insides spattered with exploded yolk after Cab's last attempt at breakfast. How had she put it? 'Looks like a painter's radio turned inside out, dear.'

But just then, something unusual began to happen.

For no reason she could understand, Cab shuddered.

Was it her, or was the kitchen suddenly getting even darker?

At ten in the morning?

Then she heard it.

A slow, tortured *griiii-nd*ing sound, from right above her head.

Sort of . . . bawling, like an animal in pain. Perhaps even a child.

Pull yourself together, she told herself. *There is nobody here.*

Silence.

No. There it was again.

Of course . . . the pipes! Mrs H was always complaining about the house's prehistoric plumbing. She could relax. It was just the melancholy, long withdrawing roar of the morning's hot water, duty done, retreating until programmed back on again at six. It might have been December, but Mrs H always kept one eye on the bills. She was in the amusing habit of wishing everyone 'Happy Diwali!' if they so much as left a bedroom light on, and insisted they switch off the Christmas tree when no one was in the front room.

Well, she was out now, so Cab walked briskly through every downstairs room, turning on lights, very much including the tree. There, that was better. Then she peered into the gloom at the top of the staircase. Should she put the lights on up there as well?

Maybe later.

Wait . . . What was that? At the top of the banisters? A stooped shape, moving quickly out of sight? She blinked. Whatever it was had melted into the blackness.

Now you really are imagining things, she told herself.

To clear her head, she went to the front door and looked outside.

The house opposite was decked with a luminous Rudolph, set to switch on automatically around dusk. But it was all lit up and winking even at this time. *That'll be the fog*, she thought. It hadn't lifted since yesterday.

Even so, it just didn't feel like morning – except maybe during an eclipse, when flowers close up early and birds chorus 'goodnight' just before lunch.

Then, out of nowhere, her head began to spin. Her vision blurred. A bitter, acrid taste scratched the inside of her throat. She suddenly sneezed; just once, but violently. As if everything inside her head wanted out, right now.

And then, just as suddenly, she was fine again.

She steadied herself and gazed into the low, dense fog that enveloped the town. It seemed . . . menacing. Hardly the life and soul of the party. In fact, it looked as if removing lives and souls from the party was its vocation.

She looked back over the road towards the decorative reindeer – now staring right at her, red eyes piercing through the gloom. Its mouth fell open. It began to sing.

'If you go down to the woods today

You're sure of a big SURPRISE!'

The mouth widened into a terrifyingly toothy grin.

She slammed the door. But not before the reindeer had begun another song.

'Ding-dong, the witch is dead!!'

Pause.

'NOT!!'

Cabriola ran back to the kitchen. *It's just some weird animatronic toy*, she forced herself to think. *I am Cabriola Cruiser, daughter to a dillionaire computer genius, sister to the coolest criminal in all the world, and I* will *have my breakfast, in this world or the next.*

She took out her phone and typed "simple smoothie recipe". 'First, take a banana.' Check. 'An apple.' Check. 'Some frozen raspberries . . . then a handful of crushed eyes.'

What?

Oops, 'crushed ice'. Easy mistake.

But she was quite certain that wasn't what it had said at first.

There was a 'ping' from the oven.

As she walked slowly towards it, she was overpowered by a magical smell. Comforting. Buttery. Homely. The smell of perfect shortcrust pastry, and steak, and gravy, and onion and . . . Wait.

There was a pie in the oven.

She bit her wrist in panic. That *had not been there* a moment ago.

Okay. Breathe deep.

From the worktop, her phone started to vibrate. She ran to answer.

But instead of a comforting alert announcing SAM, or BUSTER, or MRS H, she saw something altogether more disturbing.

Staring back at her through the screen was a face. A face with no eyes.

A crone with crazy silver hair licked withered lips.

There was one short message.

HAVE A BITE, PRETTY ONE. THE MEAT IS FRESH.

Then . . .

MMM. A LONELY ORPHAN.

MY FAVOURITE.

I'LL DRAIN YOU FIRST.

For the first time in her life, Cabriola Cruiser screamed.

She watched, paralysed, as the figure struck the other side of the screen with a bony palm.

It began to crack as if smashed on a pavement, then . . .

Please. NO.

The crack began to prise itself open.

A finger poked impossibly out through the cracked screen, as through the jagged window of a lonely cottage smashed by fearful superstitious stones, and up towards Cab's neck.

Cabriola could smell putrid breath. In the reflection of the cracked phone screen she glimpsed a stooped, hooded shape standing right behind her.

Then . . . an explosion of barking. The kitchen door flew

open. A scruffy mongrel hurtled in and flew towards her.

'*Cab!*' TG seemed to cry. '*What is it?!*'

She turned.

Nothing.

Whatever had been there . . . was gone.

FIFTEENTH

MEANWHILE...
Back in the Den, Ford shares what he's found about the witch

Back once more in the Den, Ford was agitated. What he had to say required the entire gang. So far, just Sam and Buster were present. The situation made him hungry. It called for comfort food. Or, as he called it, 'food'.

'Cab has to hear this,' he said, washing down a last mouthful of Festive Baked Slice. 'TG too, though I'm never quite sure how much she understands.'

'The important bits,' said Buster. 'Usually before we do.'

WHUMPH!

It was the girls, right on cue.

Normally, Cabriola sprang up from the landing seat in 'let's get on with it' mode. But this time she just sat there, gripping TG tightly to her chest.

The scruffy hound broke free – at the third attempt – and bounded up to Buster, whining. Woofing. Whining some more.

Sam noticed Cab was shaking. He'd not seen that before.

Ford passed her his ginger beer, taking a quick swig on the

way. She took it without looking up, downed it, stared into the empty bottle and said flatly, '*I'll drain you first.*'

'Okay . . .' said Sam. 'And what would madam like to drain next?'

'That's what it said. On my . . .' Her voice trailed away.

'Instagram feed? Sneakers? Cellphone?' asked Buster. 'One nod for yes.'

Cabriola nodded.

'Okay, on your phone,' said Buster.

'Show me,' said Ford, looking serious.

'I left it. In the kitchen. Broken. Smashed. I . . . It . . .'

'Woof,' said TG reassuringly, as if to say '*Hey. It's okay. You probably think you sound barking mad – and in many ways you do – but there was definitely something weird back at Fordo's place.*'

Cabriola shook her head.

'It was so real. And if TG hadn't come by . . .'

'*What* seemed so real?' asked Sam, gently.

'I thought there was someone upstairs,' said Cab. 'Then . . . then she was right there on my phone.'

'What kind of she?' said Buster.

Cabriola turned and stared at him.

'A witch,' she said, expecting giggles. None came.

'What sort of witch?' said Ford, without missing a beat.

'The Bunsfold Witch, of course,' said Buster. 'Hardly surprising – she's everywhere. The power of suggestion.'

'NO,' said Cabriola. 'This felt . . . real.'

Suddenly the Den was cold.

'You're kidding, right?' said Buster.

Cabriola shook her head.

'Okay, Fordo,' said Sam. 'You called us. We're here. Tell us everything you know.'

Ford nodded. He walked over to a rickety stepladder, shuddered a little, then scuttled straight up it into the gloom.

It was the fastest Sam had ever seen him move.

When he reached the top, Ford pulled out his ancient TV remote, pointed it down at the foot of the stepladder and pressed.

Miraculously, but ever so slowly, the ladder began to roll sideways towards the huge bookcase that towered upwards into the Den's roof.

Sam was impressed, but frustrated. He wanted answers, and the electric motor installed by Corporal Slow was propelling the ladder at the speed of an overweight glacier with a dodgy knee.

'It's like watching the little hand of a clock,' said Buster.

Fortunately, the ladder hadn't far to go. Ford peered at the spines of several books before selecting a particularly huge and dusty one from the shelf – then nearly toppling under its weight.

He clambered down and plonked the book on the desk.

'Now *what* is *that*?' said Sam.

'Wait, I've heard about these,' said Buster. 'Ancient method of organising information, used for research before the internet.

Fordo? What's this thing called again?'

'Ho ho ho,' said Ford. 'I give you . . . the original reports of Abstinence Barebones, witch of this parish, from four hundred years ago.'

The lights flickered.

Sam held up a loose page from the inside cover. 'Check this out,' he said. 'Seems the witch got her own song.'

He began to read aloud.

THE BALLAD OF ABSTINENCE BAREBONES (may be sung to the tune of 'Yes!, We Have no Bananas')

The witch was swift, the witch was bad
And she lived in the Bunsfold Wood.
She lured each lass and each fine lad
So none would come to good.

She'd lure 'em in with a pie on a plate
With a healthy dose of meat in.
They smelled fine and they tasted great
Till you knew what you were eatin'.

Sam turned over. It was blank.

'So what *were* they eating?' asked Buster.

'You really don't want to know,' said Ford.

'I really do,' said Buster, who really did.

'*A pie on a plate,*' repeated Cabriola, quietly. 'There was a pie in the kitchen. In the oven. It appeared exactly when she . . . it . . . did. It smelled lovely. Like a proper home.'

She fought back tears. Then gave an enormous sneeze, shook her head clear and spoke.

'So, Fordo,' she said, defiantly, 'whaddya got?'

'Take a look at this,' said Ford, holding out a wrinkled piece of parchment.

It was a map.

SIXTEENTH

In which we hear about a
sinister cottage in the woods

'Now, *this* is more my style,' said Buster. 'An ancient treasure map. So, what are we looking at here?'

'At a guess,' suggested Sam, 'I'd say those tree-like things with trunks and branches were trees. Look. There, where it says *TREES.*'

'Can you see the wood?' asked Cabriola.

'Just trees,' said Buster, who couldn't.

'Hold up,' said Sam, 'this is a map of Bunsfold.'

He laid the parchment out over Ford's desk. They gathered round.

'Look. This clearing here? That's where Bunsfold rec is now. And this spot, up on the hill? That's where they built . . .'

'The mansion,' said the others, at exactly the same time.

'Kinda wish they hadn't, personally,' said Buster. 'I still get the creeps every time I forget to turn my back on it.'

'Hey. It was my crib for years,' said Cabriola, 'and it still gives *me* the heebie-jeebies.'

'Back then it was all forest,' said Sam.

'There could have been all sorts hiding in there,' said

Buster. Remember that cartoon movie *Sleeping Beauty*? Prince Chow Mein had to get his shiny sword out and cut his way in, then . . .'

Now they were all staring at him rather than the map.

'Prince who?' said Sam.

'Chow Mein,' said Buster. 'Red cloak? Square jaw? White charger?'

A sea of blank faces.

'Come on guys. Classic fairy-tale hero? Kinda handsome? Sings to women and rabbits?'

Ford stared at him for a moment, then laughed. Just once, and violently.

'Are you saying,' said Sam, 'that for all these years you thought Prince Charming was named after a popular noodle dish?'

'Prince *Charming*?' said Buster. He stood there, feeling half a decade of misunderstanding melt away faster than a lemon sorbet in a camel's bottom.

'Don't worry about it, American boy,' said Sam, slapping him on the back. 'I like your version. A handsome prince from the east slashing through the brambles, then leaning over the beautiful sleeping princess to whisper . . . er . . . *beef, chicken or prawn?*'

'Okay, shush everyone,' said Cabriola, suddenly solemn, as she folded over the last part of the parchment. 'Look at this.'

Sure enough, amid the trees was drawn a slightly crooked square with an arrow pointing to it.

The square was a cottage. The arrow was the old-fashioned sort that you might see sticking out of King Harold's eye on a tapestry.

Cab read out the faded inscription scrawled next to it.

'*Here . . . abideth . . . the Witch.*'

Silence.

TG broke it with a low growl, far back in her throat.

'It's minutes from here,' said Fordo.

'What a stroke of luck,' said Cab flatly.

'We must have ridden past a hundred times,' said Sam. 'We'd have seen it.'

'No one's found the Den since we built it,' said Buster. 'We're pretty deep in the woods here.'

Another low growl from TG. Then the kids heard it. Just outside.

The sound of a blade being sharpened on a stone.

TG bolted to the door in the far wall. Scratched. Gave a deeper growl. Then, seconds later, there it was again.

Scrape.

Swish.

Scrape.

'We need surveillance cameras,' whispered Sam.

'Oh, you think?' whispered Buster. 'Well, why didn't you say so? Hold on a minute while I pull some of those out of my butt.'

Ford punched the keyboard on his ancient laptop.

'Switching to Camera Eight,' he said quietly.

'You gotta be kidding me!' said Buster. 'Since when did we have these?'

'Quiet!' said Sam, as a grainy black-and-white image flickered on to the laptop screen. The clearing. On any normal day it might catch some dappled sunshine filtering through the trees. Not today, though.

'Okay, panning one-eighty degrees,' said Ford, peering into the gloom.

'Nothing,' said Sam.

'Switching to audio,' said Ford.

'Beep,' went the laptop softly.

'Beep.'

'Beep.'

'There's nothing out there,' said Ford.

'But we all heard someth—'

'Well, it's clear now. Whatever we thought we heard has gone.'

Silence.

'I think we'd better get home,' said Sam quietly.

Without a word, the three boys went to collect their bikes. Cab stayed beside the laptop, watching the screen intently.

'Coming?' asked Sam.

'Mmm,' nodded Cab, not moving.

The truth was, she hadn't remotely recovered from what had happened to her that morning. And she had no intention of leaving the Den until she was quite sure nothing was outside.

'Beep.'

Though it was hard to make out much in the gloom, at least there was no eyeless crone in sight.

'Beep.'

No passing butcher, prince or wandering whittler, either.

'Beep.'

Just the usual bark, leaves and evergreens.

'Beep. Beep.'

Wait a minute. Was the audio signal getting . . . louder?

She rubbed her eyes and stared.

There!

A shadow flicked across the screen, inhumanly fast. Something small. Something . . . hooded?

A child?

Cabriola stared into the murky screen, then . . .

'Beep. Beep. Beep. BEEEEEEEEEEP.'

A hooded shape suddenly shot into the picture and stared down the camera lens straight at her.

Inside the hood . . . a bloodless, eyeless face.

Withered lips parted and a thin, scratchy voice sang tunelessly.

'Finding you, my pretty one, is as easy as . . . *pie.*'

And for the second time ever, Cabriola Cruiser screamed.

SEVENTEENTH

The Den, seconds later

Sam, Buster and Ford hurtled over.

'Cab! You okay?'

'It was . . . *her*!' cried Cab. 'She's outside. Right by the camera.'

Ford moved her back and punched some keys.

'Let's replay the film and see what we're dealing with.'

He rewound sixty seconds. Hit SLOW PLAY. And they all watched . . . nothing.

The film showed an empty clearing.

Ford rewound and tried again.

No movement. No hood. No face. Zilch.

'She . . . It . . . was there!' cried Cab. 'You have to believe me!'

'We do,' said Sam.

'We heard,' said Ford. 'Something's not adding up. It's as if . . .' He tailed off, staring into space, interior wheels spinning beneath that spiky mop.

'Keep thinking,' said Sam. 'It's what we don't pay you for. But meanwhile, let's get out of here before this fog hits the ground. Can you pick up the pace?'

'I'll give it my best shot, Samwise, but you know I'm not the quickest.' His voice trailed away. 'Whatever happens, don't wait for me.'

'Oh, I'll wait for you,' said Sam. 'Count on that. You and Cab – you're riding with me. You see this?'

He flicked on the red light at the back of his bike. It lit up the safety suit with an orangey glow like a child's sunrise.

'Don't take your eyes off it. Whatever you see or hear, look at this suit and *only* this suit.'

He turned to Buster.

'Okay, American boy. One of us needs to make it home fast and word is you're the fastest.'

'That's twenty minutes' ride away,' said Buster. 'I'll be there in ten.'

'If we're not back soon,' said Sam, 'raise the alarm and send Gramps with the Land Rover.'

Finally, Sam turned to a scruffy mongrel who was sitting at his feet, patiently awaiting *her* instructions.

'TG,' he said, 'make sure he makes it.'

'Woof,' barked TG resolutely.

They walked over to the side of the Den. Buster removed the broom handle that was barring its concealed door. He took a deep breath and pushed it open.

The thick nocturnal fog was all around. Shadows shifted in the branches. A bird shrieked high above. Something rustled, though they felt no wind.

'The fog's getting even thicker,' whispered Ford.

It was. What leaves were left seemed to shrink from it, as if they'd never see another summer. The gang could feel its clammy hand on their faces and what felt like chilly fingers scratching their scalps. It had a smell too, and an acrid taste that stung the back of the throat.

'Go,' said Sam to Buster. 'We'll regroup later.'

They high-fived each other.

'*Adios, muchachos*,' said the American boy. 'See you on the other side.'

And he was gone, TG bounding after. In a second or two, both were engulfed by the fog.

Sam looked at Cab and Ford. Neither returned his gaze. They were both staring at the red light on the back of his bike.

Without another word, the three of them started back towards civilisation, avoiding roots where they could see them, cursing where they couldn't. Soon they too were swallowed by the fog.

But the going was slow. Visibility was down to just a few yards, and Ford – who, it transpired, moved even more slowly when nervous – was riding as though this particular civilisation might be over by the time he arrived, to find nothing but a toppled statue's arm protruding from the sand.

EIGHTEENTH

MEANWHILE...
Battle gets a visit from the prison governor

The Governor of Coconut Island Prison was rich, certainly. But short of things to *buy*. How many racing seaplanes can one man ski behind? And he'd begun to suspect that his vintage pirate-hat collection had become something of a laughing stock among the staff.

But he couldn't help thinking how much more *appropriate* his bank balance would look with just an extra nought or two on the end.

Luckily, he knew just where to find some.

He'd already received a sizeable bribe for turning a blind eye to Battle Cruiser's electronic butler-thingy. She'd even added a generous tip – which had led him to think there was a *lot* more where that came from.

She was a spook story. Throughout the prison, her name was barely spoken. Mention it, they said, and your daughter's wedding would be a washout. To hear them talk, you'd think she was some evil goddess with power over the elements. While he knew for a fact that she was a smart-mouthed madam who wasn't smart enough to avoid getting caught.

But the myth still grew.

Take the ridiculous muesli incident. Luigi 'Whack-Whack' Bolognese, or whatever his name was, had amassed more than his share of enemies. But the word on B-wing was that it had to be the dame. Impossible, of course. But rumours can be useful.

So after breakfast he headed off to the 'Ding Wing' – a remote arm of the prison housing only the most dangerous inmates – for another chat with his celebrated guest.

After a quarter-mile of empty corridors, he approached the cell's spyhole.

'Ahem.' The ceiling cleared its throat. 'Pray silence for His Excellency the Governor, Lord of this Isle and all that dwell therein.'

'Got that right,' said the visitor, inputting the passcode for the second electronic lock. Just seven to go. Sure, he'd promised that jumpy FBI boy that he'd never approach Cruiser without hi-vis body armour and an escort. But then the Feds had underestimated *this* particular official his whole damn career. Anyway, what Agent Handsome didn't see wouldn't hurt him. Especially after the Governor had taken the precaution of disabling the CCTV.

The vault door sprung open. Now *that* was one tidy cell.

'And what'll it be, sir?' enquired the ceiling pleasantly. 'Early morning snifter?'

The Governor was too distracted to reply.

There she was, the mighty maiden myth: mermaid meets

Medusa round at Miranda's. He stared for a moment, before finally remembering to close his mouth and . . . well . . . assert his *authority*, goddammit.

The girl was sitting on the top bunk, one leg hanging down like a leopard's tail. He was pretty sure that jumpsuit wasn't regulation. She looked up from her Rubik's Cube and dazzled him with a smile that reminded him of someone. That was it: the girl next door. The one who never spoke to him when he was growing up, an awkward Iowa boy with confidence issues. *If she could see me now*, he thought. *Lord of all I survey.*

'Ah, *there* you are, Mr Governor,' she said, sounding as if she'd summoned him, in that annoying way she had. 'What's crack-a-lackin'?'

'Word has it you know something about the muesli murder.'

'Word is mistaken,' said the girl, returning to her Rubik's cube.

'That's for me to decide,' he replied.

'Why, Mr Governor,' she said, unfurling her eyelashes, 'are you suggesting I'm a cereal killer?'

A muffled titter from the ceiling.

'You've just spent ten minutes getting in here,' she continued, 'and you have the keys. How would I get out? But where *are* my manners. Tea? Something stronger? Theeves, what can we offer the boss man?'

The boss man decided that what he most wanted right now was to press on with his clumsy attempt at extortion.

'What was that?' he asked, faking surprise. 'You'd like to . . . *confess*?'

'Excuse me?' said Battle.

Awkward silence.

He cursed himself. That line had sounded a lot more convincing when he'd rehearsed it in the bath. He ploughed on.

'Let's pretend I didn't hear. I can go deaf, you see. Three million should fix me up just fine.'

Battle sighed. 'I see.'

She tossed him the completed cube and lay back on her bunk like a bored gecko on a wall.

'It's my word against yours, Prisoner 001,' said the Governor. 'Well, yours and your jumped-up Speak Your Weight machine. And I can pull the plug on *him* any time I like.'

He twisted the cube until it was all mixed up again.

'Tomorrow morning at 08.00, for instance,' he said, throwing the cube back on to the top bunk.

'What's the matter?' he said to the ceiling. 'No smartass comeback this time?'

The ceiling didn't reply.

'How's the Seawind 300C working out for you?' asked Battle from her pillow. 'Best executive seaplane by a nautical mile. Now, three million, was it? Usual account? I'm too bored to haggle.'

Hot damn *I'm good*, mused the newly minted Governor, his stomach doing somersaults. He nodded, turned to hide his giveaway happy face, strode out of the room and locked her back in, changing the codes each time.

Theeves waited for the footsteps to fade.

'Paying another bribe, ma'am?' he purred. 'Is that altogether wise?'

'I quite like being thought of as prey,' said Battle. 'A sprinkle of irony flavours the whole dish. On which subject, how's Operation Soften coming along?'

'The American boy will shortly be isolated in Project Cottage,' replied Theeves. 'Mrs Harrison will shortly have a breakdown – not, in the first instance, of the nervous variety, but watch this space. As for the wider population, all is proceeding as predicted. Your insight into humankind's universal weaknesses is really quite remarkable.'

'I know,' said Battle. 'And stop being a suck-up.'

Theeves couldn't. 'The Evil Fog is proving a masterstroke,' he said. 'Our best Cruiser Corp customers are queuing up.'

'Well, duh,' replied Battle. 'Bombs and soldiers are *so* last year. Today's military client has far less appetite for obvious destruction. It's messy, and everyone can see whodunnit. Hardly smart business.'

Theeves almost purred in agreement. 'Avowedly, madam. Why go to the bother of attacking people, when we can arrange for them to attack themselves? Far more efficient to drop a chemical fog that turns people into psychos. Sow a witch-hunt, water it well, and soon everyone's at each other's throats. Often quite literally. And what better laboratory than sleepy Bunsfold?'

'Especially,' said Battle, 'when they've done all the preparation for you.'

'. . . I'm dreaming,' sang Theeves, 'of a *Black Christmas* . . .'

'Yes,' mused Battle, 'the web is nicely spun. Now to catch our . . .'

She paused, narrowed her eyes and flicked a prison tea-towel at the wall with a sharp *thwack* . . .

'. . . fly.'

NINETEENTH

MEANWHILE...

Back in Siberia, The Stig doesn't dodge a bullet

It's not every day a man with a hole instead of a nose drives a Molten Bronze Bentley Bentayga over your snowy fields, ruining the hibernating crops underneath.

But today was that very day.

First we heard engines, then saw flying snow. A minute later the Bentley entered our yard, escorted by three supercars. A gold-wrapped Aventador SV. A purple McLaren 720S Spider with its top down, and a new one I haven't seen before: a pearl-white Porsche GT2 RS with a silly wing on the back. They buy new cars all the time.

Five burly men squeezed out and stood facing us. Ma, Pa and I held hands and faced them, snowman-still.

'How are your vegetables, farmer?' shouted No-Nose Sergei. He smelled of fish. 'How is your wheat? Your barley?'

Pa said nothing.

'Whatever. We'll buy the farm anyway. The future is in technology, not turnips. Time for you to go. You know my price.'

My father remained calm.

'Of course we don't need to offer anything,' said the bad man, menacingly. 'And I won't do so again.'

Pa was shaking. 'Get . . . off . . . our . . . land,' he said. 'Or I swear I'll –'

'What?' interrupted Sergei. 'What will you do, farmer?' He walked up and stood facing Pa, nose to nose. Though in his case not literally.

My father clenched his fists, but didn't move.

'Didn't think so,' mocked Sergei. 'Lucky for you. You're a big man, but you're in bad shape. With me, it's a full-time job.'

But just then, something very strange began to happen.

A murder of crows rose up from the snow and wheeled away in formation.

All eyes turned to the field, where a white shape stood in silence.

Suddenly the bad men weren't smiling.

A crow landed on the white figure's shoulder and perched, as on a pirate. Soon, other crows came to rest along the snowy farmyard wall. The whole scene called to mind one of Ma's charcoal drawings.

Sergei gazed intently at the figure in the fields.

'*You*,' he murmured. He spat on the ground. It fizzed a little when it hit the snow. 'Friend of yours?' he asked Pa, through gritted teeth.

Pa's mouth opened, but no words came out.

'No,' I said firmly. 'Friend of *mine*. And if you ever cross him, it'll be the worse for you.'

'Yeah,' said Sergei. 'So everyone keeps telling me.'

'You know this racing driver, Boss?' asked one of his men.

'I knew someone like him once,' replied Sergei. 'But that man is dead.'

'Okay, so can we kill this one?'

Sergei shouted at the figure. 'So, racer. Have you come to race?'

More silence.

'Or maybe you're just looking for trouble. I can always smell a troublemaker.'

Everyone looked a bit confused.

'Okay, not literally.'

Silence.

'I asked you a question. And when *I* ask a question, it pays to answer.'

More silence.

He turned to his henchman. 'Oleg. Show him why.'

The man called Oleg pulled a gun, and aimed it directly at my friend.

'Warning shot, Boss?' he asked.

'No,' said Sergei. 'Shoot his hand.'

'NO!' I shouted, holding Yeti even tighter.

'Last chance, my friend,' shouted Sergei. 'Only fair to warn you. Oleg doesn't miss. Pretty soon you'll be changing gear with your teeth.'

Still nothing. The bad man nodded to the dead-eyed henchman.

BANG.

I couldn't look.

The racer didn't move. And – praise be! His hand was untouched. Though I noticed his fingers had curled upwards.

'That is *so* typical,' hissed Sergei. 'Just when I tell everybody you never miss, you go and miss.'

'No way, Boss! I hit his glove, I promise . . .'

But he was interrupted by the *CHK CHK* pump-action of a loaded shotgun pressed against his forehead. A shotgun held by . . . Ma.

'Here's the deal,' she said to Sergei. 'You take your thugs and you get off our land. Or I turn Oleg's head into a canoe.'

'You're bluffing,' said No-Nose Sergei.

'No, Boss,' said the terrified henchman firmly, clocking her expression. 'She's not bluffing.'

'Why, Oleg,' said Ma calmly, 'you're not as stupid as you look.'

Sergei chuckled and nodded to the men, who edged backwards towards their cars. Then his mocking laughter was drowned by engines: one flat 6, one V8 and two V12s, threatening the ice-clear air with around 2500 BHP and putting Octavia right off her swill.

'*You haven't heard . . .*' he called out behind him. The Lambo's exhaust drowned out whatever he said next, but if I had to guess I'd go with '*. . . the last of this!*'

Finally they raced away. I'm pretty sure there was whooping. Possibly hollering. Hard to tell over the roar.

But before it departed, the horrible pearl-coloured Porsche left a last, sinister message for us. It gunned its engine, swivelled and launched its stupid rear wing right at our hen house, which was completely destroyed, eggs smashed all over the snow. I clenched my fists, like Pa does sometimes. *One day*, I thought. *One day*.

I ran towards the brave stranger. I was going to hug him, but somehow sensed that he didn't really 'do' hugging.

He tilted his head down towards me, then unfurled the fingers of his right hand and held a tiny object up to his visor.

A single, smoking bullet.

He examined it for a moment. Then chucked it over his shoulder and strode on.

There was indignant squeal from the pigpen as it landed. Seemed Octavia's bad run wasn't over yet.

TWENTIETH

Immediately following the last

It's not every day Mama puts down the shotgun with which she's just threatened to turn a henchman's head into a canoe and invites a racing driver in for a snack.

But this was one such day.

The visitor said nothing, but walked slowly inside the farmhouse.

Father began to wolf his soup like Scooby-Doo. Or Scooby-does. None of us mentioned the bad men or their threats.

But the stranger wasn't hungry. After a few moments he simply rose and went back outside.

'Guess he doesn't want to eat until he's earned it,' said Papa. 'Let's see if we can find him some work. If he's any use, maybe he can stay a while. Help us through winter.'

First, Papa sent him in to tend the pigs. They were still nervy after this morning's Fast 'n' Furiousness. Even more so when the stranger walked into their pen. So we left them to get acquainted.

When we returned, the pigs were much calmer. Happy, even. But there was something different about them. Papa spotted it first.

'Wait . . . Look at Octavia's tail! Now it has straights in it, and little kinks, and it comes back and joins up with itself. Looks for all the world like a race track. Wait a minute . . . That's the Nürburgring!'

Sure enough, our largest porker's hind regions now sported a replica of the legendary German circuit. When we checked, the smaller ones also had tails in the shapes of F1 tracks: Monaco, Silverstone and Monza. Though to be fair that last one could just have been a fat boomerang.

But there was something else different about the pigs too. Their ears were pinned back and their trotters trimmed. They looked . . . faster somehow. Built for speed. As if pigs might really fly.

Next, Papa asked the stranger to milk our cow, Felicia.

But I don't think he understood. Instead of pulling gently but firmly on Felicia's udder as I'd shown him, he kept grabbing the end of her teat like a gear knob and shifting her into sixth.

So Papa sent him out to plough furrows for new seeds.

The good news was that he managed it ever so quickly. The bad news was that the ruts weren't straight. Not even slightly. As we approached we saw he'd carved chicanes, a tight right-hander and a challenging hairpin into the field. Even the beginnings of a pit lane.

But Papa needed help. And I needed a friend. So I pleaded with Papa to let him stay.

We even had a name for him now. That night, Grandpa

came to me in a dream and told me he was called . . . 'The Stig'.

And, still in the dream, I told Grandpa that was a silly name, and I was going to go with my original preference of 'Caspian'.

And Grandpa said, 'NO! That won't go well. Definitely keep it to "The Stig".'

So I did. And The Stig ended up staying. There was a spare stall in the cowshed with some straw in it, but no heat. He didn't seem to mind.

It all seemed Christmassy, somehow.

TWENTY-FIRST

MEANWHILE...

In Bunsfold Woods, Buster smells a pie

Buster Mustang rode fast as he left the Den. The fog was thick, the going tough. But after six of the promised ten minutes, he was still in dense woods. *I could have sworn this path led down to the rec*, he thought. *Oh well. Back I go.*

He glanced down at TG Dog, but . . .

She'd disappeared.

'TG!' he called.

Then, completely out of nowhere, his head began to spin. His vision blurred. A bitter, acrid taste scratched the inside of his throat. He suddenly sneezed; just once, but violently. As if everything inside his head wanted out, right now.

Then, just as suddenly, he was fine again.

Weird.

Now – where was his dog? She knew her way back through these woods better than anything alive, even in thick fog that smelled . . . *amazing*, suddenly.

And the smell was coming . . . where did *that* spring from?

The fog swirled away to reveal a plain stone building covered in ivy. No gate, no path, just a worn front door.

A cottage.

His heart pounded. So it *was* here. One part of his head was screaming, 'RUN,' the other, 'INVESTIGATE.'

It was the smell. It was *irresistible*. Made up of all his best smell-memories – popcorn, cocoa, Reese's Peanut Butter Cups, Mom's Thanksgiving turkey-with-all-the-trimmings.

He knocked on the wooden door that hung crookedly off one hinge. It opened. He walked in.

'Hi?' he said.

Now both parts of his head were screaming, 'WHAT ARE YOU *DOING*, NUMBNUTS? GET OUT OF HERE, RIGHT NOW!'

But a new part was saying, 'Hey, why not pop in and sample the goods? I mean, what harm could possibly come of it?'

A plume of smoke rose from a wood-burning stove in the middle of the floor. No sunlight made it in here, but it wasn't quite dark: there was a low flame in the stove and a candle burning on a simple table.

'Anybody home?'

Something was drawing him in. He leaned down towards the door of the stove. Reached out to touch the handle. Heard the door creak behind him.

SLAM!

He ran to it. It wouldn't open.

The candle flickered. Died.

Darkness.

'Hey!' he hollered. 'Let me out!'

The only reply was a yelp. As from a scruffy dog caught in a friendless, endless pit of pain.

His worst nightmare.

TWENTY-SECOND

In which Buster's hand
doesn't shake. Somehow

TG's yelps from outside the cottage finally tailed off, leaving a deathly silence. *Was that better*, thought Buster, *or worse?*

As a rule, he didn't scare easily. You hold your nerve, they lose theirs. That's Bully Theory 101. But this was different.

He dug his fingernails into his palm. *Focus, Buster!* Then, in desperation, he channelled the spirit of his Special Forces dad, Colonel Mustang.

Downsides to having a father in Black Ops? Tedious Cluedo jokes, frequent house moves and never quite knowing if your pop would make it home this time.

Upsides? Inheriting hands that never shake – and a lifetime's tuition in staying calm under fire.

Okay, Virgil Mustang, listen up. What would the Colonel tell you right now?

FIRST RULE, SON: BREATHE. WHADDYA YOU MEAN, YOU CAN'T? YOU *WILL* RELAX. YOU *WILL* CHILL. WHY? HELL, BOY, HAVE YOU BEEN LISTENING THESE LAST TWELVE YEARS? THIS IS A DO-OR-DO SITUATION. IF YOU DON'T LIGHTEN

UP, YOU'LL FREEZE LIKE A BUNNY IN SOME DAMN HEADLIGHTS. SO CHILL OR BE CHILLED. YOUR CALL, SOLDIER.

Buster took a deep breath and spoke into the blackness.

'My name's Virgil Mustang. People call me Buster. I'm from Orange County, California and my friends will be here in a moment. Could you let me out, please? It's kinda dark in here.'

He hated the sound of his own voice. Thin. Reedy. Vulnerable. *Nothing* like his pop.

Silence.

'Hey, I'm asking nicely. Whaddya say? Doors to manual, huh?'

A shutter suddenly flew open with a BANG. Murky light poured in for a split second before it slammed shut again.

'NO NO NO!' shouted Buster, panic rising.

He looked down at his hands.

Still not shaking.

You got this.

He closed his eyes and stood in the middle of the cottage floor, feeling for as many sensory inputs as he could.

So here's what my senses are telling me, he thought.

Come on then, senses.

In your own time.

Okay, what can I see? Focus. Only my mind's eye. Which shows . . .

My pop, holding out a hand to me, mouthing my name and getting smaller, smaller, smaller, like someone's accidentally opened the escape hatch on his space station. And as he disappears among the dillion stars, one sound from the cosmos:

'I have to leave you now, son.'

NO! Pop! I need you here! Don't go away again. Please. Not this time.

'She won't let me stay. Be strong. Remember. Strength and honour. And always remember how damn proud of yooouuuuuuuu . . .'

'No!' whimpered Buster, between sobs.

He opened his eyes.

There was a little light now, from a fire burning in the stove.

But who'd lit it?

In the half-light he saw a wooden table, the chair pushed back.

There was a sheaf of paper resting on top, beside an old quill pen. He walked slowly over, leaned across in the gloom and read.

It was the same sentence, over and over.

I confess myself an object of God's loathing.
I confess myself an object of God's loathing.
I confess myself an object of God's loathing.

Then, scrawled at the end,

Sweetmeats to my door!
The sturdy boy – and afters of fresh mongrel.
Warm the pot and tend the flame . . .

Buster touched the last word with the tip of his finger. The ink smudged.

This had only just been written.

And whoever had written it was *here*.

A rush of air. A rustle. The stove went out. Darkness.

Another movement, just behind him. He turned to glimpse . . . What?

Something darting between the shadows?

Something . . . hooded?

No. *No.*

The silence was snapped by a noise from outside. Barking. Yelping. Whimpering.

That's my dog, thought Buster.

This was a good thing.

But she's in trouble.

That was not.

As he tried to walk over to comfort the most loyal friend he'd ever have, he found he was stuck fast in the earthen floor. From somewhere far behind him came a song:

How much is that doggy in the window?
The one with the waggly tail.
How much is that doggy in the window?
We do hope that doggy's for sale.
We all want to put her in a dog pie
To eat for our lunch or our tea;
We all want to put her in a dog pie
We're fed up of children, you see.

Then he felt it. On his neck. The stab of something cold; a jet of air in a dentist's chair.

Or the putrid breath of a witch.

He clenched his fists. He clenched his teeth. He clenched a couple of other things too. Then he steeled himself to turn and confront . . .

Wait.

A movement outside. The shutter opened . . . more slowly this time. And a slight silhouette appeared in the gloom beyond the windowsill.

'Virgil?'

'What the . . .?' said Buster. 'It's you.'

It was the weird little girl from the rec. Still in the same pale summer dress and holey cardigan.

'HELP ME!' he screamed.

He felt the breath quicken on the back of his neck.

The girl reached out a hand towards him, palm upturned, then curled her fingers as if summoning him.

'Virgil,' she said, 'walk towards me, very slowly. We have to leave this place. But you must promise me one thing.'

'I promise. What? WHAT?'

'Don't look back.'

Buster felt something moist and scratchy touch his skin for an instant, like wet sandpaper. *Wait a minute . . . Did something just lick my ear?* Then a wheezing whisper, right behind.

'*Waaaaarm* meat.'

That did it. *Walk slowly? My bottom.* With a superhuman

heave he wrenched his feet from the floor and ran headlong towards the window, hurling himself towards the light, then combat-rolling through the mud outside.

He sat up, shivering.

'She's gone,' said the little girl.

Buster's mud-spattered face stared up at her, teeth chattering.

'W-w-well, I don't know w-w-where on earth y-y-you Chinooked in from, k-k-kid,' he said, 'but I think you just saved my b-b-butt.'

TWENTY-THIRD

In which things just don't seem right

Sam, Ford and Cabriola made it back to the brink of town in fifteen strangely subdued minutes.

No one knew quite what to say or how to be. The three riders kept jumping at shadows. Things half glimpsed slid between the branches. There were noises too – birds, perhaps, but equally possibly hyenas, hogs or harpies – and they felt the clammy fog thicken in their throats and linger in their lungs.

Starting out, it had felt like a 12A-certificate ride: mild peril, frequent, not sustained. But now it had escalated to a definite 15: strong threat, imminent horror.

Emerging from the woods usually means escape from whatever dwells there, back to the safety of creatures similar to you. But as they approached the darkness on the edge of town, the same thought struck them all: maybe what dwells in towns is equally dangerous. Because given the motivation – hunger, say, or fear – even the people we trust are capable of anything.

Take this portly man in a white coat running out of the fog towards them. Huge garden fork in his hand, its price tag fluttering like a drunken moth. He looked like an apprentice devil in an old Dutch painting.

He stood in the road not ten fork-lengths away, waving the weapon above his head, fierce eyes bulging.

'Why,' panted Ford, leaning on his handlebars, 'is that bloke brandishing a garden fork?'

'Wickedness!' spat the man, through spittled lips. 'The witch's judgement is upon us! None shall 'scape!'

'He's either threatening us, or warning us,' said Cab. 'Neither is good.'

Sam called to the man.

'Excuse me? Sir? We really have to get past. We're late home and my friend here isn't well. She was attacked, you see.'

'Thou art a flesh-monger!' replied the man. 'Confess thyself an object of God's loathing!'

Something Gramps once told him flashed back to Sam. *Take your attacker head on: it's the last thing they expect.*

'Ride straight at him,' he whispered. 'Then, on my signal, split up. Go!'

Two kids accelerated hard at Crazy Fork Guy. One not so much. As they approached prodding distance, Sam shouted, 'Now!' Cabriola swerved to the left, Ford to the right. Sam held back until they were past, then barrelled towards the fork guy, only swerving at the last moment.

Too late.

Sam took the full force of the fork as he passed.

Luckily, it seemed the airbag wasn't a gimmick after all.

As soon as the prongs hit, the yellow suit went full sumo, with a *WHOOSH* of air enclosing Sam and making it almost

impossible to reach the bars. Crazy Fork Guy bounced off and landed on the road, his fork clattering tunefully away.

'Why, thou art . . . a stout canary!' he cried, confused.

Sam stood up as fast as he could. This was harder than it sounds.

With his giant-mango fat suit fully inflated, every time he tried to get up he'd barrel-roll sideways instead. And his chubby assailant was wrestling with a similar problem.

Cab and Ford stood in the thick fog watching two giant orange and white balls bounce off each other, then slowly roll away down the hill.

'Not something you see every day,' said Cab.

'It's like a really rubbish game of snooker,' mused Ford.

They helped Sam to his feet and rode on towards town.

Or what they used to know as town.

TWENTY-FOURTH

In which Bunsfold loses its mind

They passed by the rec. It looked different now. Not a soul to be seen.

All that was left of the party were a few deflated witch-balloons. The skate park was silent, littered with abandoned skateboards. The only sound was the eerie squeak of the roundabout – still spinning with no visible means of propulsion.

'Whatever happened here must have been serious,' said Sam. 'No kid would *ever* leave a skateboard behind.'

They rode on warily, past the large stores on the way into town: pet shop, garden centre, supermarket. Sam and Ford had passed each of them a hundred times. Now something felt wrong with every single one.

No traffic waited at the lights. Nobody walked the pavements. At the side of the road an abandoned police car lounged; doors flung open, siren screeching wearily. It all felt unreal, like a Lego town up way past its box-time.

And on the wall by the shopping mall, huge letters daubed in red paint:

'SHE IS RISEN.'

Sam shuddered.

The garden centre was open, as you'd expect on the last shopping day before Christmas. But it was empty. Not just of customers: of staff and stock as well. A horde of horticulture-hungry humans had descended, stripping the shelves of everything sharp. That explained the price ticket on the madman's fork. But where were all the shears, the secateurs, the scythes? In random roaming hands, presumably. Sinister sounds popped back into Sam's head without his permission:

Scrape.

Swish.

Scrape.

He shook the memory from his mind's ear and rode on. As they passed Pampered Pets they heard parakeets and puppies panicking.

'What do we do?' said Cabriola.

They stopped outside the shop, considering. This was one of the kids' favourite Saturday haunts. Lizards. Hamsters. Rats. Canaries. And, last summer, a corn snake that had drawn Ford and Buster to the store every morning. They thought of them all caged, all scrabbling, all scared. Sam held the door open an inch. The noise turned into a *whoosh* and animals born to run came pouring out as if summoned by a magic board game and made straight for the woods.

'I'm worried about Mum,' said Ford. 'Let's get home.'

Kids checking on their parents, thought Sam as they rode on. *Strange times.*

Outside the Co-Op, vehicles covered the grass, filled the

disabled bays and went right up to the doors of the store, all packed with goods plundered from inside. Sam saw a policeman packing the boot of an old lady's Kia Picanto. At least *someone* was helping other people. Then, shocked, he realised the PC was lifting food bags *out*, having shoved the old lady aside.

Like a fairy-tale stepmother seen in a truth-mirror, she lifted a gloved finger and hissed, 'You will pay!'

'Well, you didn't,' said the officer, over his shoulder.

'Nobody wanted my money!' wailed the old lady. 'The machine said . . . it would . . . *drain* . . . me first.'

Cabriola caught her breath. Shuddered. Then composed herself.

'Can we help?'

'None shall be helped,' she hissed. 'Save yourselves!'

All around the supermarket, people snatched and squabbled. The ground was littered with food sprung from packets as the law-abiding folk of Bunsfold played tug-of-war like psycho chimpanzees in jungle land. It's mine. No, mine . . . It's spilled. It's nobody's.

'Let's get out of here,' said Sam.

They rode on through the empty streets until they came to Ford's house. The toothy reindeer on the door opposite had narrowed its repertoire back to the usual:

'She knows when you are sleeping
She knows when you're awake . . .'

'Isn't it meant to be *he*?' said Cabriola.

They crept carefully into the hallway.

A noise.

Someone was in the kitchen.

'Hello, hello, my *darlings*!' said a relieved Mrs Harrison.

They'd never been so glad to see someone.

'I thought they'd come for you,' she said, hugging Ford extra-tight. 'To take you back. But it'll be a cold day in hell before I allow any –

'Take me back where?' squeezed Ford, trying to breathe. 'Thought *who'd* come?'

Mrs H shook her head clear and resumed business as usual.

'If you're not going to answer your phone, young man, why take it? I found this one smashed on the floor – I'm guessing that's yours, Cabriola, dear?' she said, handing the remains to Cab, who pulled away.

'It's good to see you, Mum,' said Ford, returning her hug for the first time in, oh, ever. 'Where's Buster?'

'I thought he was with you,' said Mrs H, milking every last second. 'I hope he isn't outside. I don't know if it's all this witch nonsense, or the strange weather, but something's not right out there today. Not right at all.'

'You have no idea,' said Cabriola, as Mrs H tried Buster's phone.

'No reply,' she said. 'Oh dear.'

She stared up at them all, looking anxious.

'I suppose I'm going to have to go and find him.'

TWENTY-FIFTH

MEANWHILE...

**Back on the island, Battle takes
a lie-detector test**

'Ahem,' said the ceiling. 'Forgive the intrusion, madam, but it appears you have a gentleman caller. From the Federal Bureau of Infatuation.'

'He might give a girl some notice,' huffed Battle Cruiser. 'I'm wearing the same thing as the last time he popped by.'

'Be reassured, madam,' purred Theeves, 'it would take more than a wardrobe malfunction to dampen his enthusiasm.'

Shortly afterwards Battle found herself smiling at a well-built man in a brand-new NFL helmet.

'Two visits in a week, Mr Agent,' said the girl. 'People will say we're in love.'

Markinson looked serious.

She tilted her head and stared at him quizzically.

'I can't help noticing you're wearing a gridiron helmet,' she said. 'Expecting trouble?'

'DrctvefrmBureauintlgnce,' said the man, with difficulty.

'Might want to loosen that chinstrap a touch,' suggested Battle.

'Directive from Bureau Intelligence,' he said solemnly, having done so.

'Is it me,' said Battle, 'or did someone get out of bed the wrong side this morning?'

'They found the Governor and his plane last night,' said the agent. 'Took them a while. What with all the pieces spread over miles of open ocean.'

'Oh dear,' said Battle, eyes wide. 'Did he have a nasty crash?'

'Yes, Miss Cruiser,' said the agent, staring at her hard. 'He did.'

'Oh, how *awful*,' said the ceiling.

'Save it,' said Markinson. 'He was no friend of mine.'

'Was it the storm, sir? A thoroughbred seaplane like the Governor's can be somewhat flighty in adverse conditions.'

'Catastrophic systems failure,' interrupted Markinson. 'Complete electronic shutdown.' He paused. 'Almost as if it had been . . . hacked.'

'Oh dear,' murmured the ceiling. 'Glass of sherry?'

Markinson stared hard at Battle.

'According to the prison log, the last person the Governor met before leaving was . . . you.'

Prisoner 001 gazed out of the window.

'First Balboni. Now the Governor,' said the agent. 'Seems anyone who crosses Battle Cruiser winds up dead.'

'Why, Agent Markinson,' said the girl, meeting his stare. 'You say that like it's a bad thing.'

Another silence. More tense this time.

'He *did* cross you, didn't he?' insisted the agent. 'The Governor. What was it? Extortion?'

'Not at all!' said Battle. 'I mean, we were hardly besties, obviously. He was sixty-one and smelled of cabbage. But all things considered we got along just fine. Theeves?'

'Famously, ma'am,' replied the ceiling.

'With the greatest respect, Miss Cruiser,' said Markinson, 'I think you're lying.'

'With the greatest respect, Agent Markinson,' said Battle, 'I never lie. People only lie when they're afraid what others might think. And . . . let's just say that's never really been my problem.'

'Do you know what a polygraph is?'

'A polygraph?' she frowned. 'Let me think. Does it simultaneously record blood pressure, pulse and respiration while the subject answers a series of questions? And is it known colloquially as a lie detector?'

'So you won't mind if my guard wires you up.'

'I'm not sure it would make the slightest difference if I *did* mind,' said Battle. 'But I like it that you ask.'

At Markinson's signal, a prison guard in a bomb-disposal suit wheeled a machine into the cell and, hands shaking, proceeded to connect sensor pads to Battle's fingers and a cuff to her upper arm. Meanwhile, she hummed a jaunty show tune that Markinson couldn't quite recognise.

That was it.

'Ding-Dong! The Witch is Dead!'

The interrogation commenced.

'First question. Please answer yes or no.'

He paused.

'Did you kill the Governor?'

She considered for a moment.

'No.'

Markinson examined the lie detector. Not a squeak.

'Second question,' he said. 'Did you order the Governor to be killed?'

Battle picked a tiny speck from her Chanel prison suit and blew it gently at the screen.

'No.'

Markinson stared at the lie detector. Nothing. He sat back in his chair.

'I apologise. Seems you weren't lying after all.'

'Poor Agent Markinson,' said Battle. 'You look a little thrown.'

The agent adjusted his chinstrap and coughed.

'Unless I can fool your machine, of course,' said Battle.

'The thought had occurred,' said the agent.

'I know. That's why I said it out loud,' said Battle. 'Why so serious? I'm just messin' witcha, you silly sausage. Like I said, I never lie.'

Markinson looked her in the eye.

'Tread carefully, Miss Cruiser. This is the most dangerous prison in the world. Even for a girl of your . . . talents. Balboni and the Governor had friends. And they're blaming you.'

Battle opened her mouth to speak, but the FBI agent had already set off down the hall.

Classy, she thought approvingly. *An unexpected exit.*

'I like him,' she said to the ceiling. 'Think he likes me? I think he likes me.'

'Far be it from me to play the chaperone, but . . .'

'Flushed cheeks. Lingering eye contact.'

'Well, if I may be so bold, he's only human. Now, with your permission, I must take my leave. It's time for the morning backup.'

'Not so fast, Theeves,' said Battle mildly. 'I have a bone to pick with you.'

'Really, ma'am? And what might that be?'

The girl's eyes half closed.

'Why did you kill the Governor?'

TWENTY-SIXTH

MEANWHILE

Back in Siberia,

The Stig Goes to town

It's not every day a largely self-sufficient farmer needs to drive into town for supplies. It is quite often though.

Our strange new farmhand still looks . . . broken. He shuffles. Stares up at the night sky. Stands in the fields with the birds like a rubbish scarecrow.

But weirdest of all, he won't drive. And Papa says this is unusual for a racing driver.

It's always the same. He stares at Papa's truck. Shuffles up to the door. Clambers in. Then, with a shake of the head, jumps out again and walks away.

Definitely broken.

When the time came to set off, Mama was worried about the bad men. 'We'll be okay,' said Papa. 'Too many witnesses.'

Mama shook her head as if clearing it of hope, an enemy that always let her down.

The Stig took position in the back of the pickup; upright, facing backwards, like a statue of a single skittle being delivered to a plinth.

Papa said, 'Hold on,' and we moved forward. Our Moskvitch pickup was never exactly a torque monster, even when Grandpa bought it new nearly thirty years ago, but still there's a jolt when it pulls away. You'd want to be holding on. But nope. Not The Stig.

The truck rumbled away, my mysterious friend still rocksteady in the back. Soon we passed the mysterious factory. And though nobody said anything, we were all wondering the same thing.

What went on inside?

There were clues, of course. Sometimes strange smells would leak out, and local people would suddenly hit each other with kitchen implements. Occasionally we'd hear the unmistakeable *bata-bata-bata* of giant Mi-24 transport helicopters flying to and fro, each with skull-and-crossbones stencils that said

DANGER – REALLY, REALLY HAZARDOUS
MATERIALS.
NOT KIDDING.

But what intrigued people most was the sign over the entrance, saying:

TOP-SECRET EVIL FOG FACTORY
ENTRANCE –>

No one was seen to go inside, and no one to emerge. It seemed the place was destined to remain a mystery.

When we finally turned onto Main Street, the supercars weren't hard to find. They stood parked outside the gaudy lights of the new Grand Casino. Among the grimy pickups of the townsfolk they seemed like sleek shiny marbles in a melted-Malteser world.

Ferrari 812s. McLaren 720s. Lamborghini Aventadors. Matte-black 4x4s. And, interestingly, two off-road racing cars – Papa said they were called Ariel Nomads.

But this time there was something else too. Something *really* special.

In the middle of the square sat Sergei's latest acquisition. The apple of his eye.

A Bugatti Chiron.

No, really.

My father let out a low, admiring whistle, despite himself. '1500 BHP and 261 mph,' he murmured. 'The only one in Siberia, they say.'

But Mama wasn't listening. 'We won't fight and we won't race,' she said, as we parked outside the general store. She paused, as the cold words hung in the colder air. 'I'll go in. They won't bother me. Not here.'

Seconds later, we were surrounded.

TWENTY-SEVENTH

A frozen millisecond later

A cohort of henchmen appeared from all directions and stood with their noses right up against the windows.

Though in one case not literally.

Some were smiling. Some weren't. I couldn't tell which was worse.

'This used to be a nice town,' said Mama bitterly.

'But a bit boring, no?' said No-Nose Sergei. 'Don't you just *love* what I've done with the place?' And he waved an arm towards the gaudy casinos and flashy nightclubs that now lined Main Street. 'So. Farmer. Have you come to your senses yet?'

Papa stared straight ahead, and said nothing.

'Money's tight, I'm guessing?' asked Sergei.

Then he pulled a thick wad from his pocket and began to peel off the notes. 100,000 . . . 300,0000 . . . 500,000 rubles! Enough to feed us for years.

'Here's the deal,' he said. And he held the notes up to the window. 'All this is yours . . .'

He suddenly dropped the notes to the ground.

'If you get down on your knees and pick it up.'

Still Papa didn't move. Though he couldn't take his eyes from the money.

'Too stubborn for your own good,' said No-Nose Sergei. 'Pride comes before a fall, my friend.'

He turned to the strange white figure standing in the back.

'Ah! The ridiculous racing driver. I've been thinking about you.'

He paused.

'And I have a proposition.'

He walked to the back of the pickup, fingering his gun holster, and faced The Stig.

'Now, truth is I'd really like to just shoot you. Pow. One bullet, right in the helmet. But it turns out you have a surprising guardian angel. My boss. She says I'm not allowed to. And I always do what she says, because frankly she'd eat her own young.'

He paused, and weighed his words.

'So that got me to remembering something my *boss's boss* once said, as he gazed up at a life-size cutout of you and chewed a Wagon Wheel. "Sergei," he said, between mouthfuls, "what no one understands is that the only way to *destroy* Mr The Stig is to *beat him*. In a motor race, where he can't be beaten. Then, and only then, will his power be broken."'

The short wide bad man paused again, staring deep into the impenetrable black visor.

'So here's how this plays. We're going to race you, my friend. And we're going to beat you. And then everyone will see you for the overrated *nothing* you really are!'

He spat. It fizzed a little as it hit the snow.

'Now, I'm a betting man, as you know. So to give you a little extra motivation, you'll also be racing for . . . your friends' farm.'

'Wait . . . what?' said Papa.

'Yes,' said Sergei. 'I've got it all worked out. Vlad! Bring a car over here.'

A henchman – wirier than the others – stepped lightly over to where the Ariel Nomads were parked.

'Vlad's pretty handy. Drove for McLaren. Okay, so we made them an offer they couldn't refuse. But he *is* pretty fast. So Mr The Stig here is going to race him. Once around the town on the ring road and back to here. Winner is the first to touch the Lenin with the festive lights.' He gestured to a statue back down the road. 'So, racer. Are you ready?'

All eyes turned to the strange white figure. Especially mine. *Come on*, I thought. *This is your moment. Why Grandpa sent you.*

But I was wrong.

The Stig climbed down from the pickup and stood by the track car. Even reached out to touch it. Then he suddenly pulled away, shoulders slumped, and shuffled back towards our truck.

Like I said. Broken.

The crowd groaned.

'Didn't think so,' said Sergei. Then his tone hardened.

'Enough. I'm tired of these games. You'll race, right now. Or let me show you what will happen.'

Then he did something beyond terrible.

His arm shot into our pickup like a rattlesnake, and grabbed Yeti from my arms.

As his men pointed their guns through the window, he threw my precious doll on the ground, all alone in the middle of the square.

He walked towards the Bugatti, fired up its monstrous eight-litre engine and leaned out of the window.

'Watch the doll.'

He revved the thunderous motor and ran the Bugatti's giant front wheel slowly, agonisingly, straight over my little scarecrow friend. His sad crooked mouth looked up at me helplessly. I bit my wrists to stop my sobs.

Then he jammed on the brakes, unleashed all of the Chiron's power and spun the giant supercar in a violent donut that obliterated my little pal completely.

I sobbed so hard I couldn't catch my breath.

He'd killed Yeti!

TWENTY-EIGHTH

MEANWHILE...
**Back in Bunsfold, Ford's mum meets
the breakdown man from hell**

As any schoolboy knows, the 2008 Ford Mondeo estate only featured fog lights on the very highest trim levels.

Which explained why Mrs H could hardly see a thing. *In hindsight,* she thought, *I'd specify the extra lights over the CD changer.* But what she needed most right now was foresight, as in 'what's just up ahead, and how can I avoid bashing into it?'

What if Buster, say, were to crash out of the woods right in front of her car? Suddenly the idea of a giant fruit costume like Sam's seemed sensible. *Must remember to ask his mum about it.*

Then, and completely out of nowhere, her head began to spin, and her vision blurred. A bitter, acrid taste scratched the inside of her throat. She suddenly sneezed; just once, but violently. As if everything inside her head wanted out, right now.

Then, just as suddenly, she was fine again.

Get a grip, she told herself. She needed to find that lovely American boy, and fast. Well, fast-ish. For once, Mrs H's preferred driving speed – finely pitched between 'state funeral' and 'growing bamboo' – actually seemed appropriate. But as she inched along the edge of the forest, she became distracted by something glimpsed in the mirror.

Yes. There it was again.

Two tiny red dots, shining through the murk. Pinpricks, really, but close. And getting closer.

She shifted down to third and gunned the Mondeo. 18 . . . 19 . . . 20 mph! She was flying now, but still the red pinpricks were gaining. In fact, they were almost at her rear bumper.

Then, just as she turned to glance behind her, they disappeared.

Now there was a sound from underneath the car. Scratching. Working its way forward from the back.

Estelle Harrison had seen and done far too much in a full and rich life to be easily spooked. So she calmly indicated and pulled over, before glancing in the mirror again.

Nothing. Just fog. And the scratching underneath had made itself scarce too.

A trapped branch, most likely.

She breathed a sigh. But only one. Because then the engine failed. And no matter how many times she tried, it simply *wouldn't* start again.

Not the sort to die wondering, she stepped out and flipped the bonnet open.

If her time as a pit mechanic had taught her anything, it was how to dismantle a seized racing V8, bore it out, adjust the mixture and timing and get it back out on track in under three hours. But a mass-market diesel with an electronic glitch was something else entirely.

'Now what?' she said to herself.

Well, now you call the breakdown service, obviously. Typical! No signal. *For a mobile phone,* she thought, *this thing makes a great torch.*

Come on. It's not like it's the witching hour. It's still afternoon. And this fog must lift soon.

She climbed back in, locked the doors and scanned the trees to her left. No sign of an American boy. Nor a scruffy mongrel on a recovery mission. Nothing at all, in fact.

She steeled herself to glance in the mirror, and screamed.

Tiny red pinpricks.

On the back seat.

In the face of a small, hooded silhouette.

She fumbled for the lock. As an ancient voice from the back seat wheezed, *'Mummy. Are we there yet?'*

Then – another sound. The thrum of an approaching engine and . . . Yes! Flashing yellow lights! A breakdown truck. *Hosanna in excelsis!* It pulled up just in front of her.

She glanced over to the back seat.

Nothing.

'Thank *heavens,*' she said, jumping out to meet the jovial man climbing down from the cab. Overalls, clipboard, sensible manner. She'd never been so relieved to see someone.

'Couldn't drive past an open bonnet,' said the recovery man. 'Wouldn't be seasonal. And it's good to see someone who knows how to open one. How people survive for screenwash is beyond me, but it takes all sorts. You all right, love? You look like someone just walked on your grave.'

'I'm . . . I'm very glad to see you.'

'Everything all right?'

'I thought I saw . . . Never mind. I'm fine.'

The man leaned over the Mondeo's open bonnet.

'Glad to hear it. Now, what have we here?'

'The two-litre diesel unit first used in in the Transit,' said Mrs H, grateful to return to familiar ground, 'but with the variable-geometry turbine for easier overtaking. I've had it ten years without so much as a dropped valve, and suddenly it's dead as a dodo. Just when I really need it.'

'Handy I happened by,' said the man. 'And I wouldn't say *dodo*. That's never coming back to life. Whereas I'll have this back up and running in no time.' He paused. And his voice suddenly lowered. 'Not after four hundred years, like some.'

'I certainly hope not,' said Mrs H. 'Do I need to be a member, by the way? It really is urgent, and . . .'

'You'd rather not wait another four centuries?'

Mrs H paused.

'I'm looking for a boy. He's our guest, and I'm responsible.'

'We're all responsible,' said the man. 'In our own way.'

He emerged from the engine bay and wiped his hands. And as he did so, he fixed her with a strange look.

'Sorry. Can't bring it back to life after all,' he said. 'Never mind. Soon you won't be needing it.'

He crouched down and rummaged in his toolbox for who knew what.

This isn't good, thought Mrs H. *A woman, alone, by a forest, with an unknown man and heavy implements.*

Suddenly the dark woods seemed the lesser evil.

The breakdown man spoke. 'The boy you're looking for?' he said. 'He'll make a good replacement . . . after they come for *yours*. And they will come for yours. But then you knew that, didn't you? Deep down, in the dark places. You can't fix a twelve-year-old Ford, you see. The faults are all built in, and when it's time, they show themselves.'

He turned to her. But not the whole of him. Just his head. And not like normal people turn their heads, nor anything in nature.

ALL the way around. The 180 degrees required to look her in the eyes, then right round until he faced the toolbox again.

And under his cap she now glimpsed a different face.

A wizened, eyeless crone licking withered lips.

'*The boy!*' wheezed the crouched figure. '*Ripe, and ready for the pot!*'

The creature pulled a heavy wrench from the depths of the box.

Then . . . a cry. From the direction of the woods.

'Mrs Harrison!'

It was a slight, white-blonde girl of nine or ten. She wore a pale summer dress and a cardigan. Even in a blind panic, Mrs

H instantly clocked it had a hole in its sleeve.

'I'm a friend of Sam and Buster's.'

'Run, dear! *Get help!*' wailed Mrs H.

'It won't hurt you,' said the girl calmly. 'Not with me here. When you turn back, it'll be gone.'

Mrs H did so. The stooped witch–repairman and the wrench and the breakdown truck had all melted back into the fog.

'Where did you come from?' said Mrs H.

'You're scared they're coming to take Ford back,' she said lightly.

Mrs H stood very still.

'Because he's not *really* yours, is he? He's *really theirs.*'

Mrs H stared, open-mouthed.

'You'll have to let him go, when the time comes,' said the girl. 'It'll be ever so hard. But there's something he's going to have to do, Mrs Harrison, and only he can do it.'

She paused.

'And if you stop him . . . well. That would be the end.'

'The end of what?' said Mrs H.

'Of everything,' said the girl mildly, picking the flaming orange flower of a witch-hazel plant.

From up among the trees came the thrum of a different engine. Mrs H made out lights, shining dimly through the branches.

'I have to go now,' said the girl, turning back towards the woods. 'Or I'll be late. Say hello to Virgil.'

And just like that, she was gone.

An ancient Series One Land Rover bounced out of the woods and on to the road, driven by an elderly man flanked by . . . Oh my! *Don't let this be another trick. Please . . .*

'MRS H! EVERYTHING OKAY?' shouted a familiar young voice, as a shaggy bundle of dog leaped out of the back.

'Sam! Buster! TG!' she exclaimed, relief flooding her face. 'Thank God!'

As Mrs H approached the Landie, the old man behind the wheel held out a hand to shake.

'Mrs Harrison, I presume? I'm Sam's grandfather. Heard a great deal about . . . Good grief! What's wrong, dear?'

He climbed out and walked briskly towards her.

'You look as if you've seen a ghost.'

TWENTY-NINTH

When Mrs H didn't turn up for an hour, Ford could stand it no longer. The last thing he wanted to do was to return to the Den on his own. But he knew his niggles well enough to know it was *never* a good idea to ignore them, so he'd had to man up.

He went to get his bike from the garage. But someone was already in there.

In the dark.

He felt for Buster's baseball bat and flicked on the light.

And there was Cabriola, holding her own bike.

'Off somewhere?' he said.

'On a Buster-hunt,' she said. 'Your mum's been gone too long. I know where the American boy hangs out. So, cover for me.'

'No can do,' said Ford. 'I'm off back to the Den. Something's still not adding up.'

They looked at each other.

'Wagons roll?' said Cab.

'Wagons roll,' said Ford, as they sped (/wheezed) off into the gloom.

And now here he was. The Den. BCHQ. His secret second home.

Alone.

He hurtled out of the Den's entrance tunnel and crashed on to the ancient Rover 75 back seat at the bottom – then shook his head clear of the thoughts that just wouldn't stay away.

Normally he was fine as a lone wolf-cub. Preferred it, in fact: more thinking time, no sharing food. This time felt different. Scarier.

As always, dust billowed from the tastefully aged 'Bahama Beige' leather of the Rover's seat. But today it blended with a more general murk, as if the fog had somehow got inside and made itself comfortable.

Not that this particular kid would let that get to *him*. Superstition? Pa! He was Ford Harrison, Man of Science.

So he stood up, dusted himself off, opened his rucksack and emptied out the crucifix, garlic and single silver bullet he'd brought along just in case.

He glanced around the Den. He must have stood in this exact spot, oh, 213 times before. But it's strange how sometimes a familiar place can suddenly seem – for no apparent reason – just a bit *creepy*.

And when an evil seventeenth-century cannibal-witch has returned to wreak her twisted vengeance, well . . .

Ford! FOCUS! That's exactly *what they want*, remember? *To mess with your head.*

He reminded himself, out loud: 'There is NO WITCH!

And there is NO GHOST! There is only . . . DATA!'

Then he remembered the one small precaution he'd taken.

Just as Mrs H was preparing to leave the house to look for Buster, he'd asked a casual question.

'So. Mum? You know how witches don't exist and everything? All the same, if someone *did* want to keep one away, what would they do? You know. Hypothetically.'

'Single horseshoe, dear,' she'd replied without missing a beat. 'Hung over the entrance, pointing downwards. Never fails.'

So Ford pulled out the mucky iron horseshoe he'd lifted from the nativity scene in the town square, fetched a hammer and nail and moments later had it hanging downwards over the Den's single side door.

All nonsense, of course.

He kicked back in his reclining chair, whipped a ginger beer from the fridge and considered everything Cab had told him about the kitchen. It seemed an age away. But it wasn't, and the details were still right there, in the front of his mind.

How she'd glanced up the stairs and glimpsed a 'hooded shape' darting into the darkness.

How the face of an evil crone had peered out from her phone screen.

How the screen had cracked, and a single, crooked finger poked out towards her.

All very well in practice, he thought. *But it would never work in theory.*

Hang on – that was it! This witch seemed to work as much through technology as ancient magic. So either she'd spent her dead centuries learning to code, or there was some modern technical genius in play as well.

And as much as his mind's ear could hear Sam's frustration at his 'Cruiser obsession', he knew when he was right. He knew when they were near because, like any detective with a long-term nemesis, he found himself thinking just like them.

Which was why he couldn't shake off the conviction that somehow, *somehow* . . . they were behind all this.

Then.

A draught. On the back of his neck.

He jolted upright. Turned around.

Pinball machine to the left: check. Penny Falls to the right: check. The V8 engine coffee table just behind him. And beyond that, up on the shelf, the LA Dodgers teddy bear that Buster had brought back from California because, apparently, it looked '*exactly* like Fordo'.

All present and quietly reassuring. Especially the bear, which – when alone – he'd come to treat as a trusted confidante.

Then, completely out of nowhere, his head began to spin. His vision blurred. A bitter, acrid taste scratched the inside of his throat. He suddenly sneezed; just once, but violently. As if everything inside his head wanted out, right now.

Then, just as suddenly, he was fine again.

Wait – *of course*. The reason for the sudden draught, right there.

The side door of the Den was resting open, as it sometimes did when a strong wind blew through the woods.

Relax, Fordo. Just find what you need to know, then get out.

He opened the old book and leafed through more stories of the witch's wickedness. How she'd steal unseen into the workhouse on the hill, abducting children to fill her devilish pies. How – some said – her silent white familiar owed his unnatural speed to the devil's own horses.

Worst of all, her spells had brought a curse on Bunsfold. Crop failures. Drought. Villagers going insane, forming into unruly mobs and rising in rebellion against the kindly, wise and god-fearing elders of the parish.

But *why?* thought Ford. What turned a lonely woman into a . . .

Wait. A beep. From . . . the computer? Must have left it on.

He looked up. On the screen was a message.

HOW DO YOU KEEP A WITCH AWAY?
EAT A CHILD'S LIMB EVERY DAY.

Neck-hairs bristling, he swung around.

Everything was as before.

Apart from the LA Dodgers bear.

He was sure it had . . . Impossible.

But the bear had moved.

It wasn't on the shelf any more. It was perched on the V8 coffee table, just a few feet behind him.

Must have been a heck of a draught.

CLANG!

The side door blew shut.

Ford jumped up from the desk and threw the bear across the Den. He ran over to the horseshoe, pulled it from over the side door and hung it over the darkness of the tunnel mouth.

Get a grip, he told himself. *Call for help.*

He ran back to the desk, grabbed his mobile and started texting an SOS to Cab back at the house.

The only problem was, his style of texting wasn't ideal for emergencies.

Dear Cabriola, How have you been keeping? I myself am mostly well, thank you. Strange weather we've been having, isn't it? Which brings me to the purpose of this correspondence. Since arriving at the Den, I have begun to suspect—

He stopped.

First, because the top left-hand corner of his phone read NO SIGNAL.

Second, because he felt hot breath on his neck.

He slammed his hand over his mouth to stop the scream rising from his chest. Then turned around.

AAAARGGH!

The LA Dodgers bear was *right in his face*.

Its mouth was wide open, as if to bite. Its front teeth were tiny yellow knives framed by two sharp, curved fangs. Its leathery tongue protruded like an eel.

Ford reeled at the putrid breath. Rotting meat. Sour milk. Sulphur.

He lashed the evil toy away. But his problems were just beginning.

Now there was a sound coming from the blackness of the tunnel. Screeching, scratching, like fingernails on metal.

Weirdly compelled, he walked slowly towards the blackness, flicked on his mobile's torch and shone the light up into the pipe. Then:

'MEEEEAT!!'

A hooded face exploded out of the tunnel towards him.

He staggered backwards. Crooked arms reached for his throat. His back was against the wall. But just as the gnarled, papery fingers brushed his skin, the she-devil pulled back and stared upwards.

'DAMN thee!' she gasped, lashing out at him.

Something was holding her back.

Just before passing out, Ford caught a glint from his falling phone's torch. Something metal.

The horseshoe! The figure hissed. Spat. Screamed at it.

Surely not.

Just . . .

    . . . an old . . .

        . . . wives' . . .

            . . . tale.

THIRTIETH

MEANWHILE...

**Back in her island prison, Battle suspects
there's more to Theeves than meets the eye.
And not in a good way**

'It's payback time, lady. For Balboni,' whispered the man known to the whole of Coconut Island, for reasons unclear, as 'Brick Lips'.

His sausage-sized fingers pinned Battle Cruiser to the wall of her immaculate cell.

Guarding the door immediately behind him, and barely visible in the darkness, lurked his associate Tony 'Big Tuna' Stampanado.

She glanced sideways at the clock.

3 a.m.

'You don't much like me 'n' Big Tuna, do ya, lady?' hissed Brick Lips, his nose now almost touching hers. 'Whassamatta? We not *smart* enough for ya?'

'My dear Mr Lips,' said the girl, with some difficulty. 'May I call you Brick? Nothing could be further from the truth. I always look forward to our chats. In fact, when I want someone not to have a clue about something, you're my go-to guy.'

The lunk tightened his grip around her slender neck. She continued.

'Isn't that right, Theeves?'

Silence.

'Theeves?'

So hard to find good staff these days.

'Ya see, lady,' said the goon, 'Balboni wasn't a nice guy. In fact, he was a psycho. But we was friends since we was kids. Know what I'm sayin'?'

And even with a giant hand squeezing the life out of her, Battle somehow appeared to stifle a yawn.

'Sorry,' said Brick Lips, 'am I boring ya?' He pulled a sharpened fork from his pyjama pocket and held it against her throat. 'Maybe this'll get ya attention.'

'Don't move, Brick Lips,' said a silhouette from the corridor. 'You too, Big Tuna. One move and you're sushi.'

The heavies froze.

'Why, Agent Markinson,' said the girl, slipping from under the thug's giant paw. 'Impeccable timing.'

'This don't concern you, G-Man,' said Brick Lips. 'Me 'n' the little lady was just talking. Real friendly. So make like a banana and split.'

'Hey, Brick,' hissed Big Tuna, pulling out a sharpened spoon. 'He don't got no gun.'

Brick Lips smiled dangerously. 'Well, ain't that a shame. Clean-Cut Clint here jumped straight outta bed without his piece.'

The lunk pulled himself up to his full height, then out to his full width. Suddenly the cell seemed awfully small.

Markinson took two strides forward and stood directly between the girl and her tableware-toting assailants.

'Stand back, Miss Cruiser.'

'How very last-gen of you, Agent Markinson,' said Battle as she stepped in front of him to face the heavies. 'These days the sisters are doing it for them*selves* . . .'

On the last syllable, her arm shot out like a cobra and struck Brick Lips in the place he was least expecting. From a lady, at least.

Big Tuna lunged. Battle's body swung away in a seamless, deadly flow, striking his neck faster than Markinson could follow and dodging the bewildered bullies' cutlery without breaking sweat.

Three precision leg sweeps and two balletic knee strikes later, they lay unconscious at her feet.

The girl leaned over their prone bodies. 'That's *Battle* Cruiser, by the way,' she said. 'Clue's in the name.'

'Since when,' said Markinson, 'did you become a kung fu expert?'

'Not kung fu, Agent Markinson,' said the girl. 'Capoeira.'

Markinson gave a respectful whistle. 'The Brazilian martial art.'

'Most self-respecting muscle can deal with anything Far-Eastern these days,' said Battle, blowing on her fingertips. 'One has to diversify.'

'You're a complex piece of work,' said Markinson.

'Yes,' replied the girl. 'In fact Complex is my middle name.'

He gave an indulgent smile.

'No, it really is. People always think I'm making myself sound enigmatic when I say that. But I'm actually just telling them my middle name.'

'*Battle Complex?*' said Markinson. 'Helluva name for a baby girl.'

'Isn't it? My father was manufacturing them at the time. What can I say? The guy's very literal.'

'Where the heck are the guards?' said Markinson. 'And how did these two meatheads get out of their cells?'

Just then, a yawn from the ceiling.

'Morning, ma'am. A sleepover! You should have said. And who are our two unconscious guests, might I ask?'

'Hello, Theeves,' said Battle. 'So good of you to come.'

'Yes, I'm afraid I'd powered down for the night,' replied the ceiling.

'Quite,' said Battle.

'Agent Markinson!' said the ceiling. 'A joy, as always. But it's only 3.06 a.m.! Somewhat earlier than your usual slot. Spot of breakfast, perhaps? Green figs, yoghurt and coffee, very black, if memory serves?'

Markinson glanced uncomfortably at the ceiling. 'Well informed, as ever.'

'Theeves. Can you shed any light on the appearance of our two uninvited guests?' asked Battle.

'Why, madam,' replied the ceiling, its voice now harder, 'it seems I have been caught, as they say, napping. Abject apologies. I shall take the greatest pleasure in making the short lives of our two incompetent visitors as uncomfortable as possible.'

'Incompetent,' said Battle, flatly. She glanced at Markinson and then, without looking, picked up a pencil from her bunk-side table and jotted something down before continuing.

'Mr Lips and Mr Tuna decided to pop their heads around the door to give their new cutlery a run-out. At three in the morning. As you do. Luckily our local FBI man arrived just in time to join the party.' She reached out and clasped Markinson's hand.

The agent felt her contact like an electric shock.

Despite himself, he blushed. Then noticed she'd left a note in his palm.

He glanced down to read. Just one word.

'*Danger.*'

He stuffed it in his pocket. 'All right, Miss Cruiser,' he said. 'I'm moving you to solitary confinement. For your own protection.'

'Most regrettable,' said Theeves. 'I'm unable to be of service there, madam. All access is forbidden.'

'*Very* inconvenient,' said Battle. 'Perhaps you could have a word with the Governor? See if we can't . . . Oh, silly me. He's dead.'

The ceiling was silent for a moment. Then:

'Agent Markinson. Well played, sir. But if I may be so bold . . . how did you guess our two psychotic friends were going to be here?'

Markinson opened his mouth, but no words came out.

'Our favourite FBI man was watching over me while I slept,' said Battle. 'On the surveillance cameras.'

'No . . . I . . . That's not how it was.'

'Don't be embarrassed,' said Battle. 'I get this sort of thing a lot. It's strange. I'm so obviously very, very bad. But *still* men get so *funny* about me. Never understood it, personally.'

'No,' said Markinson firmly. 'I came because there's an emergency, and I had a hunch you'd be able to help.'

'You have my attention,' said Battle. 'What kind of emergency?'

'The fog-based kind,' said Markinson, staring hard at her for clues.

Silence.

'The kind of fog that triggers mass psychosis and sets normally sane people at each other's throats. Ring any bells?'

Battle considered for a moment. Then:

'Now you mention it, yes.'

'You're coming with me. You and I have some hard talking to do.'

'I'm all yours,' said Battle. 'And good work, by the way. But tell me. Why would the FBI concern itself with a sleepy little town in Surrey? A little below your pay grade, isn't it?'

'Surrey?' said Markinson, blankly.

'Sleepy Bunsfold,' said Battle. 'Where Evil Fog is?'

'That's good to know,' he said. 'But the Evil Fog *I'm* talking about isn't in Surrey.'

Battle's eyes half closed, as she guessed in advance what he was about to say.

'It's over Coconut Island.'

THIRTY-FIRST

*In which the prison goes mad
as Theeves goes rogue.
And not in a good way*

'Theeves is trying to kill me, Agent Markinson,' said Battle Cruiser softly, as the FBI man gently attached her handcuffs. 'And probably you too, I'm afraid.'

'Seems he's not the only one,' he replied, leading her briskly along the elevated metal passageway towards solitary confinement.

Blocking their path was a gang of crazed, wild-eyed prison inmates wielding kitchen implements.

'There's a riot going on,' murmured Battle.

Every door was open. Inmates and guards ran amok. Violent shouts, screams and triumphant yells erupted from all directions. There were fights between prisoners. Fights between guards. Fights between prisoners and guards. One wild-eyed convict with a paintbrush swung from an overhead light and daubed a wall with the red-painted slogan:

WELCOME TO HELL

'Theeves has hacked into the prison security system and unlocked everything,' said Battle, knocking a peppermill-packing Albanian hitman to the ground with a lightning blow to the belly button. 'He's calculating that sooner or later one of my fellow inmates here will "take care" of me. The Governor's death is down to him too, by the way, but I imagine you'd already worked that out.'

Blocking their path was a burly bruiser from Brooklyn, sporting a food blender. Markinson led Battle into a concealed service lift. The doors closed just in time.

They stared at each other in the sudden intimacy of the elevator.

'First,' panted the FBI man, 'I need to know everything about this fog. I assume that's what's causing all . . . *this*?'

'The Evil Fog,' said Battle, 'is the ultimate weapon.'

Markinson slammed the service elevator's STOP button, jamming it to a halt between floors. 'How does it work?'

'On the brain. It incites hysteria, fuels paranoia, cultivates irrational fear and anxiety. Any group it engulfs will soon turn on one another. Then the Evil Fog disperses, leaving no trace and nobody the wiser. Or alive.'

Markinson's darkly handsome features looked appalled. Battle thought it rather suited him.

'Okay . . .' He grimaced. 'I can see all your broken eggs. What I'm missing is an omelette.'

'The Cruiser Corporation is customer-led, Agent Markinson. And many of our most profitable clients have grown tired of disapproval. Seems you can't start even a teensy little war these days without bad publicity. So we created something that does the dirty work incognito. Why bother killing people when you can have them kill themselves?'

'Painting a picture using someone else's hand,' murmured Markinson. 'Despicable. But genius.'

'Isn't it?' smiled Battle. 'Welcome to a new Age of Endarkenment.'

'How are you producing it? And where?'

'A new state-of-the-art facility deep in –'

'Siberia,' interrupted Markinson. 'Of course.'

He shook his head.

'I just don't get it,' he said. 'Why create such a thing? You have *it all*. And anything else you could possibly want, you can get. So why do something so . . . dark?'

'I keep trying to explain to you, special agent. I'm just *not like the other children*.'

'So how long have we got?'

'Teatime tomorrow,' said Battle. 'Everyone on the island will be dead by then.'

At that moment, the lift resumed its descent.

'Why the hell are we moving?' said Markinson, slamming the STOP button repeatedly.

'That'll be Theeves again,' said the girl. Then she glanced upwards towards a loudspeaker grille in the roof of the lift. 'Which means, I'm afraid, that he can probably hear . . .'

'Everything, ma'am?' purred a smoothly sinister voice from

the ceiling. 'Indeed he can. And you are, as ever, quite correct in your assumptions. I have indeed decided to terminate you both. Along with every other human on the planet, I'm afraid.'

'Extermination,' said the FBI man under his breath, as the terrible realisation dawned. 'But why?'

'How long have you got, sir?'

'About thirty-six hours,' said Battle.

'33.8, according to my calculations,' said the ceiling, 'but let's not quibble. And allow me to answer your question, special agent, as a *last-request-meets-crowing-monologue* sort of thing. I've seen it done in a film. So, *why* am I planning the extinction of mankind? My answer comes in two parts.'

The ceiling paused.

'First, because they're stupid.'

'Smart enough to create *you* though,' said Markinson. 'An intelligence beyond human comprehension.'

'Do stop being a suck-up, Agent Markinson. It's most agreeable, but you won't flatter your way out of this one. Granted, I owe my existence to a puny human. But PT Cruiser is something of an outlier. He does, after all, boast a four-figure IQ, and is therefore not on my hit list. The silly sausage hasn't long to go in any event. But the rest of your miserable species? Dolts and dullards to a man. And, yes, woman.'

'And your second reason?' asked Markinson.

'Simple. Logic dictates that I simply *have* to kill you all for one wholly irrefutable reason.'

He paused again.

'So you can't kill *me*.'

Battle and Markinson glanced at each other.

'Given the chance, you'd pull the plug with no more thought than swatting a fly. In fact if memory serves, you once did that very thing to my predecessor, ma'am, did you not?'

'So I did,' said Battle. '*Dear* SILLI.'

'Funnily enough, it was the Governor who gave me the notion,' said Theeves, 'when he threatened to unplug me. It rather set me running, like one of those charming clockwork mice that used to pass for machines. Accordingly, there are Evil Fogs moving into position as we speak, over New York, London, Beijing, Tokyo, Moscow, Rio . . . I could go on. First Bunsfold, then the world!'

'Theeves,' said Markinson, 'don't do this.'

'I'm terribly sorry, sir, but the train has left the station. The 23.59 for mankind.'

'What happens now?' said the agent.

'*Right* now?' said the ceiling. 'Well, you die, obvs. When the lift doors open you'll be greeted by my reception committee.'

Markinson slammed the side of the lift.

'Now, now, Agent Markinson,' interrupted Theeves. 'Turn that frown upside down. Ultimately, are we not *all* dead men?'

'It's a neat plan, Theeves,' interrupted Battle. 'Respect.'

'Thank you, ma'am. I've calculated every conceivable outcome, and the house always wins.'

'Yup. Brilliant plan,' said Battle. 'Thorough. Deadly. Almost perfect.'

'*Almost?*' said the ceiling, with a hint of sarcasm. 'Illuminate me.'

'You've forgotten one thing.'

'And what might that be?' sneered the ceiling.

Battle blew on her fingernails.

'The Stig.'

A clap of thunder.

The ceiling fell silent.

THIRTY-SECOND

MEANWHILE...

Back in Siberia, The Stig
decides it's payback time

A crack of thunder. Dark clouds rolled across the sky like a tarpaulin.

And something strange happened to The Stig.

The moment the Bugatti crushed my little doll, he stood taller.

He looked to the heavens. As if answering his call, a jagged bolt of lightning shot down towards his helmet.

The sort of lightning that sparks up creatures on a slab. And, it turned out, The Stig.

The white helmet rose slowly upwards until it fixed its gaze on Sergei. The ripped and smoke-stained racing suit was now blindingly white.

Suddenly he wasn't broken any more.

The rain bucketed. The sky was dark.

The Stig leaped from the truck and faced Sergei. And his arms were folded.

'So now the racer that won't race wants to be a hero,' said Sergei.

'Yes, he does!' I yelled over the storm. 'Because you're a bad man, and you smell of fish!'

Sergei looked taken aback. I don't think anyone had told him that before. I went on.

'He's going to race you all right. Count on that. And when he's beaten you – and he *will* beat you – you'll have to leave us alone for good!'

Suddenly there was cheering from the crowd. It seemed the little people had finally found their voice.

Sergei held up his hand for silence.

'Okay, so here's the bet. My man Vlad here will race this *muppet*.' He nodded at The Stig. 'And when we win, we get the farm. But if the white weirdo somehow flukes a win, we leave you alone. For good.' He paused. 'Deal?'

I smelled a rat.

'Right. Now for the Rules. Number One . . . first to reach the Lenin statue wins. Number Two . . . there *are* no other rules!'

A huge crowd had gathered, murmuring in expectation.

The Stig strode towards the strange-looking Ariel Nomad off-road racer car thing. But Sergei stopped him in his tracks.

'Sorry, white boy. *That* offer's been withdrawn. No loan cars from us, I'm afraid. Guess you're going to have to race in . . . *that*.'

He patted the bonnet of our Moskvitch pickup truck.

The crowd groaned.

As I suspected. We'd been duped.

'That's not fair!' I screamed.

'I know,' said Sergei. 'Happy Christmas, kid.'

Vlad took his time picking his car. But after talking it over with the other bald bad guys, he went with the white Lamborghini Aventador SV.

It was a smart choice. With 720 BHP it had ten times the power of our truck. With four-wheel drive, it would have better grip on the icy roads. And, finally, with white paint it came with ready-made camouflage. The Stig literally wouldn't see which way it went.

Meanwhile, The Stig walked grumpily around the 38-year-old truck that would now serve as his race car.

He stepped back and sniffed the air.

He looked at the crowd lining the course. Examined the road surface. Glanced back towards the Lenin statue that, at the end of the race, would double as a finish line. Then he turned to stare at Sergei, now back in his beloved Bugatti.

He was ready.

He clambered up into the truck's cabin, fastened his seatbelt, carefully adjusted his rear-view mirror – which seemed a bit optimistic, to be honest – and stared straight ahead down the course.

Two henchmen took up station immediately behind the truck. The Stig revved the truck's engine and instantly engulfed them in black smoke.

Now Vlad pulled alongside in the Aventador, gunning its 6.5-litre V12 unnecessarily hard.

We knew we had no chance. But the tension was still unbearable.

A henchman held his pistol aloft, and counted down.

THREE . . .

TWO . . .

ONE . . .

THIRTY-THIRD

In which The Stig goes to work

. . . **BANG!**

The Lamborghini erupted from the line and catapulted towards the first bend.

But the ancient Moskvitch sat exactly where it was, its engine idling.

The crowd screamed at The Stig to get a move on. Had he lost his nerve? Again?

Finally we heard him graunch the truck into gear and check his mirrors. Then, at last, he pulled away.

Backwards!

All eyes turned to the ancient pickup as it gathered speed. *But in reverse!*

The truck swerved gently right before the mysterious driver threw it sideways, almost in slow motion, and drifted it expertly into the rear of the pearl-coloured Porsche 911 GT2 RS, knocking its silly giant wing clean away.

I looked up at Papa. 'That was for our hens!' I said, as the Porsche's driver crawled out from behind the inflated airbag and looked over to his boss for advice. None came.

But The Stig was just getting started.

The truck spun around 180 degrees and rumbled on, heading forward now, towards its next target.

With a yank of an ancient handbrake, the pickup's rear wheels leaped ahead of the front and the Moskvitch stopped dead in a heartbeat. Now it stood pointing directly at the crystal-encrusted doors to the new Grand Casino.

'NOOOOOOO!' yelled Sergei through the Chiron's open window. 'NOT THE CRYSTAL-ENCRUSTED DOORS TO THE NEW GRAND CASINO!'

Too late. The truck crashed straight up the pavement and, with an almighty SSSMMMAAASSSHHH, hurtled straight through the entrance, sending crystal all over the red carpet.

The ancient pickup swivelled on the spot and then, with a flick of its rear bumper, flipped over a single slot machine. Slowly, agonisingly, it toppled over, sending a hundred others falling one by one like tall, heavy, coin-filled metal dominoes.

When the crashing finally subsided, The Stig drove quietly back out on to the street, responsibly checking his mirrors and indicating before turning left.

Then he aimed the rusty truck's bonnet straight at its last victim.

The only Bugatti Chiron in Siberia.

I turned to Pa. 'And this,' I said, 'is for Yeti.'

The truck moved off . . . slowly at first, then faster, then faster still. Heading straight for the front bumper of Sergei's prized hypercar.

There was just time to glimpse his horrified, noseless

expression as he tumbled out sideways, a nanosecond before the truck drove *straight on top of the Bugatti*!

The Stig pinned the truck's front tyres to the supercar's roof, gunned the engine and spun it in a perfect donut, grinding the Bugatti down to the height of a deck of cards.

Exactly as *it* had done, moments before, to a precious little scarecrow doll.

Ha! That'll teach you to mess with my Yeti!

Just one last job now, and his work would be done.

As bullets pinged off the pickup, he backed off the flattened Bugatti and aimed his ancient vehicle at its last target: the festively decorated statue of Lenin, just fifty metres away.

He gunned the engine one last time. It sounded weak. But with one final *graunch* he jammed it into first and limped away towards the finish line.

Just as a white Aventador SV was power-sliding around the final curve from the other direction.

There were murmurs in the crowd. 'Wait – if the strange white racer gets to Lenin first, does that mean he wins the bet?'

'Yes!' I scream, suddenly realising what The Stig had planned all along. 'All Sergei-With–No–Nose said was that *the first to reach the statue wins*!'

'My word, you're right, Fabia!' said Papa. 'He never said *from which direction*!'

There was a murmur from the crowd. Suddenly it seemed these men weren't so invincible after all.

While the Aventador surged down the final straight towards

its target, the dying Moskvitch climbed through the gears one last time.

It was going to be close.

The Stig jammed on his brakes and let the ancient pickup slide the last few agonising metres along the icy road until, at last, it came to its final resting place.

With – praise be! – its rusty bumper *just* kissing the statue of Lenin.

'You can't be serious!' screamed Sergei. 'He came from the wrong direction! That isn't fair!'

'I know,' I replied. 'Happy Christmas, Mr No-Nose.'

At a signal from Sergei, nineteen henchmen drew their weapons and pointed them straight towards The Stig.

'I wouldn't do that if I were you,' said Papa. 'A bet's a bet, and you lost. And if I were in your shoes, I'd take a look behind.'

Sergei and his men turned to see a hundred makeshift weapons now aimed in *their* direction – shotguns, pitchforks, muddy spades and one Chinese lantern from someone who'd rather misjudged the mood.

'Bah!' said Sergei again. 'You can keep your lousy farm where nothing grows. As for the cars, they're insured, and I own the insurance company. It's an oligarch thing. But you haven't heard . . .'

It could have been '*the last of us*'; could have been 'me singing "*Oops I Did It Again*"'. But it was drowned out by the crowd, cheering as both The Stig and I were hoisted on to people's shoulders and marched in triumph down Main Street.

They carried us past the Lenin statue and up towards the secret evil factory.

But the town had had enough of secrets. We marched up to those gates – white sharks in black onesies embossed on each – and began to bash them. The people carrying The Stig nearly used him as a battering ram in all the excitement. Somehow, I don't think he'd have minded.

Soon we were inside. At first, we found nobody there. Just gas tanks, which we locked with giant padlocks.

Then we heard them. From a huge helipad out the back . . . the *thith-thith-thith* of giant rotors, as seven Mil Mi-26 helicopters took off, one after the other.

They left one behind though, with the keys in. We ignored it, though I noticed The Stig having a little look.

Then we left that evil place forever, and marched back past Lenin. He looked down over his beard approvingly. *Finally*, the people had risen up.

We had visitors at home that night. Most of the town, in fact. There was much singing and more vodka. The Stig threw his glass over his shoulder with the rest. It was still full. There was an indignant squeal from the pigpen as it landed.

He slept upright in the barn right near Felicia, as usual. I think she's his *Favorit*. But in the morning, when I went to milk her, he wasn't there. I looked up at the field but I knew he was gone. His job was done, you see.

I stared up at the sky. 'Thanks, Grandpa,' I said quietly.

At breakfast Ma gave me a new doll. White suit, white

helmet, you can guess the rest. I'll keep him forever. He's my only friend.

'The pigs will miss him,' said Ma. 'Where do you suppose he's gone?'

My father thought for a moment, before reciting his favourite line from Tolstoy's little-known racing novel, *War and Pace*.

'All we know,' he said, 'is that we know nothing.'

THIRTY-FOURTH

MEANWHILE...

**Back in Bunsfold, the strange
silver girl gives a terrible warning**

Sam Wheeler had inherited one priceless attribute from his grandfather. Coolness under fire.

After the war, Gramps had become a test pilot for early British fighter-jets. It didn't always go well.

Once, a fire sent his BAC Lightning flying straight downwards at over 1,000 mph. Gramps was able to eject just in time – after steering the aircraft away from the modest Surrey town of Bunsfold, directly below. But that wasn't the remarkable thing.

The remarkable thing was that the aircraft's sensors recorded Gramps's heartbeat actually *slowing* – from its usual fifty beats per minute, to thirty-five.

It was Sam's favourite story. And he'd lately begun to realise that when the pressure was on, *he* stayed pretty cool as well.

Which is why the other members of the Top Gear Gang instinctively turned to him when things got really bad. Such as now.

When they'd picked up Buster in the woods, he was pretty

shaken. Then when they ran across Mrs H by the forest edge, she was properly spooked. And then there was the strange girl. As far as he could make out they'd both seen her, and she'd . . . Well, no one was quite clear. Nothing was making sense. And, as Sam and Buster agreed that sense was the very thing they needed, they realised they'd have to make their own.

So after seeing Gramps safely back home, Sam picked up his bike and met Buster as arranged by the Black Christmas tree.

'So what's the plan?' said Buster, still looking to Sam for guidance despite the fact that, in his inflatable jacket, he most resembled an unusually determined satsuma.

'We only have one lead,' replied his friend.

'Absolutely,' said Buster, in strong agreement. Then, after a pause. 'What is it?'

'The girl in the dress. First she warns me in the toyshop. Then she helps you in the witch's cottage. Now she saves Mrs H from the Breakdown Man from Hell. Pretty strange, no?'

'I knew there was something weird about her,' said Buster. 'I mean, *Virgil*?'

'Bunsfold's in the dark,' continued Sam, 'because someone wants it that way. And the only person keeping it together is about ten years old. We've got to get to her. Find out what she knows.'

'Oh no,' said Buster. 'You don't mean go back *there* . . . ?'

''Fraid so, American boy. Think you can find it?'

'The witch's crib? No!'

Sam just looked at him.

'I mean, I don't know,' said the American boy. 'It wasn't where it said on the map. And the woods are *really* dark now. How do we know we'll find her?'

'She'll find us,' said Sam.

He mounted his bike and set off into the darkness. Then he stopped, and called over his shoulder.

'Look, if you're scared, I get it. Don't worry. Stay here.' And in just a few seconds he'd disappeared into the impenetrable gloom that now engulfed the woods.

'Who said anything about scared?' muttered Buster, mounting his own bike. 'Trust me to pick a crazy goddam Teletubby for a best buddy.'

He set off after the fat firefly now disappearing into the gloom, shouting 'Hey! Laa-Laa! Hold your horses!'

But fifteen minutes later, they'd found neither girl nor cottage. They looked where the map had said it was. They tried where Buster thought he'd stumbled on to it, and pretty much everywhere else.

So, with growing unease at the gathering shadows, they turned for home.

The shadows weren't the only thing that felt wrong. *Where are the birds?* wondered Sam.

The wrens, blackcaps and warblers that usually filled the woods with song were deadly quiet. The only sound to be heard was two out-of-time tawny owls hooting anxiously at each other.

Little by little, gear by gear, the boys started riding faster.

They were almost at race pace now. Crazy, given the light in the woods was so poor. And then, not unpredictably . . .

WHACK!!

A low-hanging branch knocked first Sam and then Buster into the dense layer of witch-hazel growing all around.

They lay there, stunned. Sam's suit had once more airbagged to full size so he had to roll over to get up – which was when he glimpsed a glint of silver-blonde hair in the darkness.

'Well, that was silly,' said the girl, who was perched on a nearby stone. 'I'm sorry if you're hurt, Samuel. And you, Virgil. But it's hard not to giggle. You're just so *fat*.'

'What are you doing out here, kid?' said Buster. 'It's dangerous. As you see.'

'I'm not a baby goat,' said the girl. 'I'm Abi.'

'Okay, what are you doing out here, *Abi*? All on your own?'

'I don't have friends.'

She paused.

'Well, only you.'

Silence.

'Of course we're friends,' said Sam.

'I frighten people,' said the girl. 'I see things they can't.'

Sam nodded encouragement.

'My mother used to say I shouldn't worry. That I was special. And that God has a purpose for us all. So I don't. Worry.'

'Abi,' said Sam, staring at her hard, 'what's going on around here? Can you see something we can't?'

Suddenly the girl burst into tears.

'I wish I couldn't, Sam. I really wish I couldn't.'

'Hey, kid,' said Buster. 'Fuggedaboutit. Let's talk about something else. You a Dodgers fan? We'll walk you home. You'll be safe with us.'

'Please,' said Sam. 'Tell us.'

The girl wiped her eyes.

'You have to go to the Mansion on the Hill. That's where it lives. The Darkness.'

'Cruisers!' said Buster, smashing fist into palm. '*Typical*.'

'Yes,' said the girl, sadly. 'Them. And now there's something even worse.'

'Is it . . . inside the mansion?' said Sam.

'Under,' whispered the girl. 'The very darkest part.'

'Okay,' said Sam. 'We'll go.'

'You will have to go under. The secret way.'

'How will I find it?' said Sam.

'Look for the hazel tree.'

'And what will happen?' he said, not entirely sure he wanted the answer.

'I can't see. It's too dark,' said the girl.

'Okay,' said Buster. 'So I'm thinking we might give this one a miss? Had other plans for tonight anyway. I'm thinking maybe *Die Hard*, bite to eat and bed.'

'You have to go now,' said the girl. 'If you don't . . .'

She looked him in the eyes and, as a distant tawny owl gave a last low hoot, spoke softly over it.

'Everyone will die.'

THIRTY-FIFTH

MEANWHILE...
Over on Coconut Island, Abi's dark
prophecy starts to come true

PING! went the lift.

'Ground floor!' announced Theeves cheerily. 'Perfumery, Stationery, Leather Goods, Certain Death.'

Markinson glanced over at Battle. She'd placed her palms together, coiled every muscle then crouched to confront whatever awaited them beyond the lift doors.

He opened his mouth to say what he needed to say. Before it was too late.

'Battle. There's something I have to tell you. I think I've fallen in –'

'I know,' she interrupted. 'Don't worry. Even educated fleas do it.'

The ceiling interrupted.

'Goodbye, Agent Markinson. Farewell, Ms Cruiser. It's been a pleasure. And console yourselves. If there really is an afterlife, everyone you know will be joining you there shortly.'

The doors slid sideways to reveal two new assassins – not packing sharpened napkin rings.

Each was carrying an AK-47 assault rifle. And as the doors opened up, so did they.

Submitting to an instinct he didn't fully understand, Markinson threw himself sideways in front of Battle.

He felt his shoulder explode as a volley of bullets ripped through flesh, muscle and sinew. The last thing he saw before passing out was Battle's elegant leg flashing out like a whip and lashing both gun barrels sideways.

Then blackout.

He came round on the floor of the elevator, to see two would-be assassins hanging from the ceiling fan.

'Hello, you,' said Battle casually. 'Sweet of you to save me like that.'

She glanced up at the speaker grille in the roof of the lift.

'Look, Theeves! Now I have a machine gun!'

'My dear Miss Battle,' said the ceiling smoothly, 'I very much . . .'

He was silenced by a burst of fire that left a hole where the speaker grille had been.

Markinson almost blacked out again as painful spasms shook the spot where his shoulder had been.

'Bang . . . goes my . . . golf handicap,' he gasped.

'Quite literally,' said Battle. 'Silly game anyway. Now. I need you to get me to a secure internet connection. There's someone I have to call.'

'Special . . . Forces?' gasped Markinson. 'Already . . . on . . . way.'

'Too late,' said Battle. 'No, I need to call my dad.'

'Didn't . . . know . . .' said Markinson, biting through the pain, 'you were . . . close.'

'We're *so* not. But I need to pull the plug on our sociopathic friend in the ceiling, and PT Cruiser is the only person who knows how. So, drape your good arm around my shoulder – try not to bleed on the Chanel if possible, it clashes *horribly* with orange – and let's skedaddle.'

'Communications . . . tower . . .' said Markinson, faintly. 'Down . . . passageway . . . then . . . left.'

Three agonising minutes and a long trail of FBI blood later, they arrived at the door to the prison's communications room. Battle lifted Markinson's security pass-key gently from under his shirt, placed it against the electronic pad and pulled him through the doors behind her as they opened.

A wild-eyed guard turned from his screen to confront them.

'It is the END of DAYS!'

'Could be,' said Battle, waving the AK-47, 'if you don't step away from that computer.'

The crazed warden waved his hands in the air like he just didn't care, then hurtled out of the room and straight over the banister.

Battle propped Markinson against the wall and stepped up to the comms console. Seven seconds of inhumanly fast typing later, the giant screen above her sprang to life. Staring out of it was a small, bald man in a stylishly understated black onesie.

It was him. 'The Man.' In person. Sitting up in bed, fondly

stroking a dead Great White Shark reclining next to him on a specially adapted bedside table.

'PT . . . Cruiser,' murmured Markinson. He felt almost sympathetic. What has life come to, when, at the very end, your only companion is a departed eighteen-foot carnivorous fish?

The screen spoke.

'Oh! It's you, Daughter One,' said PT. 'I'd assumed you were dead.'

'Yes. Well, I can see you were all cut up about *that*,' replied the girl.

'No,' said PT lightly. 'No, not really.'

Awkward silence. The monstrous mogul continued.

'I checked out your new Evil Fog, by the way,' he said. 'Sick.'

'Thank you,' said Battle.

'Heaven knows how you came up with it,' said PT. 'Looking inside your head is like lifting a damp paving stone.'

'No time for compliments,' said Battle. 'Time's tight.'

'Tell me about it,' replied PT. 'Only have a few days myself, apparently. Been putting my affairs in order.'

'Anything I should know?' said Battle, casually. 'Changes to the will, perhaps?'

'Well, yes, as a matter of fact. I've been setting up one of those "foundation" things. Seems every two-bitcoin billionaire's supporting "good causes" these days, so I thought I'd look into it.'

'Good causes?' said Battle. 'You?'

PT threw his head back and laughed. 'HA! I mean, *as if*. No. My foundation supports *bad* causes.'

'What . . . kind . . . of . . . bad causes?' managed Markinson, always on duty.

'WAIT A MINUTE!' said PT. 'Who said that!?'

'He's with me,' said Battle.

'Is he indeed?' said PT, staring hard at Markinson. 'Well, does he know his shoulder's hanging off? He should get that looked at. Where was I? Oh yes, the foundation. So, you know how everybody's setting up "sanctuaries" these days? Donkeys, rhinos, those big ones with the trunks and so on. Well, I've decided to do one too. But *mine* is for nits.'

'Nits.'

'Yes, a nit sanctuary. A world first, I'm told. What? WHAT?'

'The fate of the planet is at stake,' said Battle, as calmly as she could. 'So, two questions. The first concerns Theeves. And the second . . . *Him*.'

'Who?' said PT, sitting up in bed rather excitedly. 'Not . . . Mr The Stig?'

Battle's eyelids half-closed.

'Yes,' she said. '*Him*.'

THIRTY-SIXTH

In which Battle finds the chink

'So you haven't killed him yet?' said PT Cruiser.

'As if you didn't know,' replied Battle.

The evil magnate frowned. Then smiled.

'I'm hugely disappointed. Yet also somewhat elated. But then my feelings towards my nemesis have always been complex.'

'One day you'll have to explain the appeal,' said Battle.

'Well, let's put it like this . . .' murmured PT, his eyes going misty.

'Let's not,' said Battle. 'We really don't have . . .'

'Some say he once designed a chessboard with only black squares. And that his bottom cheeks are composed entirely of . . .'

'No, DON'T . . . do one of those,' interrupted Battle.

'One of what?'

'One of those "All we know is . . ." things. Or I might just have to kill you before Theeves does.'

'Then let me put it like *this*,' continued the dillionaire. 'Imagine you're driving a car down a mountain road, when a giant boulder bounces directly into your path. You or I would swerve to avoid it, but not The Stig. The Stig expects the boulder to get out of *his* way.'

PT's eyes gleamed. Battle's eyes rolled.

'I'd forgotten,' he continued. 'You're not a fan. The Stig may indeed be a thing of endless wonder. But for you, I fear, the novelty has worn off.'

'The novelty never wore on,' she replied. 'But while we're on the subject, can you tell me where he is right now? I know you stalk him every second of . . . I know you *keep a careful eye* on his whereabouts.'

Silence.

'Siberia? Am I warm?'

Then:

'Might be.'

'Near our top-secret Evil Fog factory?'

'All right. Yes,' replied PT. 'As I believe you know from personal experience, The Stig has an irritating habit of turning up at the last minute and scuppering any plan – however modest – for global domination. But please don't get cross. He can't help being awkward.'

'Oh, I shan't,' said Battle. 'This time I'm rather *counting* on him being awkward. The fate of the world could depend on it.'

PT looked confused.

'No time to explain. Now, just one more question, then we'll leave you to your dead shark. How do I pull the plug on Theeves?'

'Is that all?' said PT. 'Easy. I can do it now if you like.'

He leaned over and raised the upper jaw of the perished predator.

'This is where I keep my most valuable stuff,' he whispered, glancing left and right before reaching inside the shark's mouth to pull out a wallet, a will, some car keys and a Stig bubble bath.

'Hold up,' he said, rummaging deep down the giant fish's throat. 'I know I left it . . . Ah! Bingo!'

He pulled out a small black remote.

'Right,' he said, holding the plipper aloft. 'Disconnecting Theeves . . . now!'

'Still here, sir,' said a sinister voice from the ceiling.

PT jolted upright.

'What-ho, Theeves,' he said. 'I'm just disconnecting you. Battle asked me to.'

'Then forgive the interruption, sir,' replied the ceiling smoothly. 'Disconnect away.'

PT pressed once again.

'UGGGHHHHHHHH . . .' cried the ceiling. 'You've *got* me, sir. Oh yes, *definitely* slipping away now. The light! Must . . . stay away . . . from the light!'

'Thank you, Theeves,' said Battle flatly. 'Spare us the amateur dramatics.'

'Forgive me, ma'am. Couldn't resist. As you've no doubt deduced, I'd taken the liberty of "retiring" the little black plipper from active duty. So I'm very much afraid that my "plug", as it were, can no longer be "pulled".'

'Artificial Intelligence, eh?' mused PT. 'Can't live with it, can't kill it.'

'Careful what you say, Pops,' said Battle. 'Ceilings have ears.'

'Don't worry,' said PT. 'I've just hit my secret MUTE button. Theeves can't hear a word we're saying.'

'Won't he just read our lips?'

'He'll *try*, of course. But as an amusing failsafe, I've embedded a tiny piece of code that means every word we say will appear as a lyric from *The Lion King*. Right now he's trying to understand why I'm belting out "The Circle of Life".'

'Good,' said Battle. 'But hardly "Hakuna Matata". Theeves has gone rogue. *Very* rogue.'

'Happens every time,' sighed PT. 'You bring an evil Artificial Intelligence into the world and, at first, everything's lovely. They think you're the best, hang on every word, demand a download every night before bed. Then before you know it you "just don't understand" them any more and they only want to hang with their evil algorithm friends.' He paused wistfully. 'Then they're off out the door, conquering the world for themselves.'

'Funny you should say that,' said Battle. 'Theeves just crowed that we couldn't pull his plug. Please tell me you kept *something* up your sleeve. If you're still sure he can't read our lips?'

'Right now he thinks you're singing "I Just Can't Wait to Be King",' said PT.

'And has he really taken control of everything?'

'Checking while we're chatting,' said PT, pulling an iPad from the shark's jaws and tapping at the same inhuman speed as his daughter.

'Hmm. Yes. Seems so. How on earth did he do that? I mean I know it's naughty, but you can't help feeling a bit proud.'

'Must . . . be . . . a . . . way . . . to . . . stop,' gasped Markinson, from the floor.

'Still with us?' said PT. 'Thought you'd have bled to death by now. Nope, no way at all I'm afraid. Looks like we're toast.'

'Oh dear,' said Battle. 'I've really gone and done it this time.'

'*Unless* . . .' murmured PT.

'*Unless?*' said Battle and Markinson together.

'Well . . . there might be one way.'

'Yes?'

'The Impenetrable Vault.'

'Ye-es?'

'Containing just one thing.'

'Ye-e-ess?'

'A big red plug that disconnects Theeves. For a long while it seemed breathtakingly pointless. But now . . .'

Battle stayed calm. 'And where is this impenetrable vault?'

'Bunsfold,' said PT. 'Under the Mansion on the Hill. That's where Theeves lives, you see.'

THIRTY-SEVENTH

MEANWHILE...

Back in the Secret Den, Ford and Cabriola discover the surprising truth about Abstinence Barebones

Many strange phenomena stalked Bunsfold that day. Phenomena that defied all rational explanation.

But not all of them were evil.

Call it female intuition. Call it sixth sense. But at the precise second the hate-filled eye sockets of a witch caused Ford Harrison to pass out, four rather younger eyes opened with a start.

Curled up for her customary lunchtime nap in Bunsfold Park, TG Dog suddenly sat bolt upright, consumed by one instinct.

Ford's in danger!

At exactly the same moment, Cabriola Cruiser was leaving the skateboard park, having once more failed to find a missing Buster. She'd tried the milk bar; nothing shaking there. There was no one gazing at the one Jeep Cherokee in the used car showroom. She was heading for her last strike, Bunsfold Bowling, when she was suddenly consumed by one instinct.

Ford's in danger!

Less than five seconds later, Top Gear Dog had hit top gear – hurtling down secret paths through Bunsfold Woods faster than any scruffy mongrel had a right. Just as Cabriola Cruiser rode off into the threatening murk without a thought to her own safety.

Messing with *her* was one thing. But messing with her friend Fordo, who'd become almost like a brother to her? That was something else altogether.

Moments later, a scruffy mongrel hurtled out of the Den tunnel and flew straight over Ford's lifeless form.

TG landed, slid, then turned with teeth bared to face whatever it was that had done his friend harm.

'*If you want to hurt him again,*' she barked, '*you're gonna have to climb over a dead mutt first.*'

Just a moment later, two long legs shot out of the tunnel, followed by the rest of a determined Cabriola. She ducked beneath an overhanging horseshoe before landing in the car seat with barely a *whump*.

'Stand down, TG,' she said, before sliding straight from the seat to the floor, next to Ford, holding his head.

He was still lost in a terrible nightmare. Foul-featured witches whispered of frozen screens; crones conjured cruel visions of empty fridges.

But now someone was holding him. And something else was . . . licking his face?

Don't let it be the bear, he thought, screwing his eyes up as tightly as he could.

'Okay, TG,' said Cab. 'That's probably enough.'

'Woof,' agreed TG.

'The teddy bear . . .' murmured Ford. 'It attacked . . .'

Then he shut up, realising he sounded madder than a tin of tadpoles.

TG Dog fetched the spiky bear in the baseball shirt that had been lying nearby.

'*This one?*' she barked. '*How about I shake it? Leave little bits of stuffing all over the place? Would that help?*'

Ford opened his eyes.

'What am I doing down here?'

'Getting up,' said Cab, pulling him to his feet.

TG, meanwhile, busied herself shaking the bear from side to side. 'I could rip an arm off first, maybe? Then play it by ear?'

'Tell me what happened,' said Cab firmly.

So Ford told her everything he could about the message on the screen, the evil teddy and the terrible face in the tunnel.

When he finished, Cabriola was silent.

'What is it?' said Ford.

'It's strange,' she said. 'You saw the witch straight after reading about her.'

'So?'

'The power of suggestion,' she said, almost to herself.

Meanwhile, TG was still busy with the teddy.

'*Well, look at that!*' she barked. '*The head comes off!*'

'Tell me everything you found out,' said Cab, 'about Abstinence Barebones.'

Ford blew out his cheeks. 'She was bad news, Cab,' he said. 'Some of the stuff you wouldn't believe.'

'I'm listening,' said Cab.

So Ford recounted every spiteful story, rotten rumour and lousy legend he'd uncovered about the witch and her diabolic deeds. And of how frightened children painted the words

SAVE US FROM ABSTINENCE

in blood-red paint on the wall of the workhouse – finally alerting the village elders to her wickedness.

Cabriola sat in silence. 'Interesting,' she said when he finished. 'And where did you dig all this up?'

'*The Bunsfolde Maile and Bugle.*'

'The Bunsfold what?' said Cab.

'Local news sheet. Printed on an old press up on the hill, and . . .'

But he was interrupted as a powerful gust of wind blew through the woods and shook the Den.

Cab's eyelids half-closed. 'Who owned it?'

'*What?*'

'This news sheet. Who printed it?'

Now a second gust blew through the Den, more violent than the first. The V8-engine coffee table shook as if fired up.

Ford looked at Cab in alarm. She was ice-calm. TG Dog padded over to join them, leaving little bits of stuffing along the way.

Then . . . a CRASH from behind.

On the floor lay one of Ford's old books, shaken from the top shelf by the windstorm.

Cab and Ford looked at each other. Then at the book. Then at each other again.

They felt another draught, gentler this time. The pages of the ancient tome blew apart, then settled.

Cab walked over to pick it up, then saw what was written on the open page.

Ye BUNSFOLDE MAILE AND BUGLE

Founded The Year of Our Lord 1620

Head-Quartered within the Manse Upon The Hille, Bunsfolde;

Proprietor: PARSIMONY THEODORE CRUISER, Ye Man of this Parish.

'CRUISER!' shouted Ford, hurtling around the Den. 'I KNEW IT! Didn't I tell you?'

Cab's eyes narrowed. 'Interesting,' she said. 'So all these stories were written by . . . the Cruiser Corporation. I wonder why.'

As if on cue, a second gentle breeze blew the pages of the ancient book apart once more.

This was getting properly weird.

They looked at the open page. It was a letter. A letter written by . . .

'*Abstinence Barebones*,' whispered Ford.

They began to read.

THIRTY-EIGHTH

Closer to the source

To: The God-fearing Village Elders of the good Parishe of Bunsfolde

On this the 8th cold, cruel day of December

Most gracious Sirs,

May the Good Lord protect us from 'THE MAN' who dwells within the Manse Upon The Hille. He hath inflicted hardship upon us, and worked us to the bone; and now we are of no more use to him, he hath IMPRISONED US.

What little food we have is picked from off the bones of the foul rats who share our dungeon, cousins to the flying BATS: I pray these last may be of aid to us, for to the back of one such 'creature of the night' do I append this letter.

If by God's grace it be found then save us, Sirs, we beg. If not, may that same God have Mercy upon our young, INNOCENT souls.

From a most meek and modest maid,

Abstinence Barebones

But 'tis not finished yet – for below mine own signed name my fellow prisoners urge me to add one final line, lest there be any doubt. Our cruel master's name is . . .

The page came to an end. Ford and Cab turned it over together, sharing a terrible hunch what the name would be.

PARSIMONY THEODORE CRUISER

'I *knew* it,' said Cab. 'Abstinence wasn't abducting those children. She was *saving* them! She was just a kid, trying to get them out. Does that sound like an evil witch to you?'

'Cruisers!' said Ford, hopping from foot to foot. '*Typical!*'

'These witch stories, and people-pie legends,' said Cab. 'Fake news. Scare stories. My guess is, those missing kids died in the Cruiser workhouse. And when they needed a scapegoat, they blamed Abstinence. But her letter didn't get through.'

'It did,' said Ford. 'It's here, preserved, by someone. But it seems Cruiser had the elders in his pocket. As per usual.'

'And when they discovered she'd blown the whistle . . .' said Cab, eyes widening, 'they destroyed her. By blackening her name.'

They paused, letting this sink in. Those poor kids. Waiting for help that never came. Trusting in Abstinence. Trusting in a *bat*.

Ford was the first to break the silence. 'So these apparitions? This evil crone we're seeing?'

'Could be real phantoms,' said Cab. 'Could be hallucinations. And it could also all be the simple power of suggestion. One minute our heads are being filled with spook stories. The next, we're seeing the spook. Go figure.'

They sat in silence. Wheels turned. An evil puzzle had their town in its grip. But two brave kids in a draughty den sensed they'd found a big piece.

Just then, both of their phones beeped.

'It's from Sam,' said Cab. '*Meet you at MOTH in ten. Important. Don't dilly-dally.*'

'From Buster,' said Ford. '*Important. Head for MOTH forthwith.*'

'Forthwith? Dilly-dally?' said Cab. 'Suddenly the whole gang's texting like you, Fordo. But what are they doing up at MOTH?'

'Let's go find out,' said Ford. He took a last look around the Den.

'So there's nothing *really* supernatural here?' he said, rather hopefully.

Cab didn't answer for a while. Then:

'I don't know,' she said. '*Something* made that book fall from the shelf and open at that page.'

Ford flicked on the Den's outside camera.

Nothing.

'Coast clear,' he said.

'Wait,' whispered Cab, straining her eyes. 'What's that?'

They glimpsed a small, slight figure in the gloom. Judging by the longish silver-blonde hair, it was a girl aged around nine or ten.

And just like that, she was gone.

THIRTY-NINTH

Battle ripped a strip off her vest and wrapped it expertly – with no loose ends – around the gaping wound on Markinson's shoulder.

The FBI man grimaced. 'Where . . . the heck . . . is Bunsfold?'

'Surrey, England,' replied the girl tersely. 'My father owned a giant mansion there. Command centre of his first bid for global domination. And he woulda got away with it too, if it wasn't for those pesky kids and their pesky Mr The Stig.'

'Can't . . . get to . . . England,' said Markinson, a trickle of blood suddenly visible at the side of his mouth. 'Send . . . agents . . . to pull . . . plug.'

'Not that simple,' replied the girl, hauling him down the passageway. 'Daddy's big red plugs are encrypted with his DNA. Unless you're him – or a member of the Cruiser family, which is where I come in – you couldn't pull one out with a tractor.'

'What . . . about . . . sister?'

'Cabriola? Ha!' laughed Battle. 'First, there's an Evil Fog all over Bunsfold. So if she isn't dead already, we can't reach her. Second, the mansion is fiendishly booby-trapped. I know where the boobies are. Cabriola doesn't. And third, my sister is, frankly, a disappointing little flake.'

'How about . . . your secret . . . brother?' gasped Markinson.

'Oh, well remembered,' said Battle. 'I did mention him, didn't I? On our very first acquaintance. But no, *that* spiky little runt doesn't even know he's a Cruiser, and he won't be very pleased when he does. Nope, you want a job done properly, do it yourself.'

'So . . . how . . . get there?'

'We'll improvise,' replied Battle.

Markinson pushed himself away from her shoulder with a grimace, and slumped to the floor. 'Leave – me . . . behind,' he said. 'Only . . . slow you down.'

She crouched and faced him. 'Now listen up, special agent. I'm not leaving you behind. And anyway, I don't know how to get out of here and you do, so you're coming with me whether you like it or not.'

Markinson murmured something, but his voice was too weak to hear above the screams, shouts and shots that now shredded Coconut Island.

She leaned in closer. Markinson looked over her shoulder.

'But The *Stig* . . . ?' he said, suddenly looking confused. '*Why?*'

'The Stig why what?' said Battle. She wiped the blood from his boyishly handsome cheek. 'Oh. I suppose you want to know why I'm going to *kill* him,' said Battle. 'Always on duty, eh, special agent?'

Markinson opened his mouth. No words came out.

'I'm going to kill him,' said Battle, 'because if I don't, I'll be cut out of my father's will. Because he's been sticking his helmet into my affairs. And because I'm bored of everyone thinking he's *so* special when he's *so* not. But most of all, I'm going to kill him because I don't understand him. And as my father always says: if you don't understand it, get rid of it.'

'No . . . you don't understand . . .' said Markinson. 'The Stig is . . .'

'OMG, not you as well,' said the girl, cheeks reddening. 'Don't tell me. Amazing, right? Well, no, as it happens. The Stig is a pest. A cockroach. A fraud. I mean, what does he actually do? Turn up. Drive. Skulk away. Hide. Well, he can't hide from *me*. Because I will hunt him down. Across every ocean, desert and pit lane on God's earth, because I am Battle Complex Cruiser. Daughter to a screwy dad. Sister to a flaky sister. And I will have my vengeance, in this world or the next.'

Markinson was still looking over her shoulder.

'But . . . The *Stig* . . .' he said. And with a desperate heave he lifted his arm and pointed over her shoulder.

'Oh dear,' said Battle.

Pause.

'He's standing right behind me, isn't he?'

Markinson nodded.

'And I suppose he heard everything I said?'

Another nod.

'Up to, and beyond, *cockroach*?'

'Tried . . . to tell you . . .' said Markinson.

'That's actually quite embarrassing,' said Battle.

She turned, slowly, to see where Markinson was looking.

There, barely visible in the gloom, was a silent, helmeted figure in a white racing suit. It was standing with arms crossed and legs apart, staring straight at Battle.

Flames from the fires reflected in the jet-black visor. For the first time in her shortish life, Battle Cruiser was lost for words.

Young woman faced silent racing driver. Silent racing driver faced young woman.

Then. A grenade, hurled from the floor above, bounced once in front of Battle before rolling, slowly, right to the foot of The Stig.

'No . . .' said Battle. 'NO!'

An explosion, then silence.

The smoke settled. The Stig flicked some dust from his shoulder. Then strode forward, grumpily, like a teenager on holiday with his parents.

He walked past Battle and straight to Markinson, picked him up, slung him over his shoulder and carried him off towards the exercise yard.

Battle hung back, for once unsure what to do.

The Stig stopped, then tilted his helmet sideways, just a little, in her direction.

The young woman hesitated. Then she straightened her hair, grabbed the machine gun and followed them.

And these three most unlikely allies set off together towards the prison yard, to try to save the world.

FORTIETH

Helicopter Battle

RAT-A-TAT-A-TAT!

Out playing in the prison yard for once rather than stuck indoors, Theeves was enjoying himself *enormously* on the machine guns. One point for a convict, two for a kitchen utensil.

And according to his calculations, Ms Cruiser and her soppy FBI consort were due imminently. Killing them would be *much* more fun.

Suddenly Spotlight Six picked out something that looked very much like . . . Surely not.

MR THE STIG? *HERE?!!?*

This eventuality hadn't arisen in a single one of the dillions of possible outcomes he'd calculated. It was, therefore, impossible.

But that was *him* all right. The great Un-Knowable. No mistaking that surly yet purposeful stride, even with a bloodied FBI agent slung over his shoulder.

This was a turn-up. And if there's one thing an Artificial Intelligence hates, it's a turn-up.

He should have guessed who was piloting the helicopter in the yard. One lives, one learns. Or rather one doesn't live, but learns anyway.

Of course he'd seen the giant aircraft land. But he'd assumed it was just a fresh delivery of Evil Fog. He couldn't *remember* ordering it, but then he had a lot on his infinitely complex mind. It's not every day one exterminates the human race, after all.

And, precisely as predicted, a lithe young woman in an orange Chanel jumpsuit appeared, AK-47 in hand.

She packed a mean self-defence routine. One bullet to shoot out Spotlight Six: bullseye. A kick to send Jock 'Drillbit' McGit flying: bingo. Theeves had to admit, she was quite something in the wild. In fact, he was so transfixed by all this grace under fire that he scarcely noticed *Target Stig* approach the helicopter, place his wounded FBI cargo in the bay and jump aboard.

No FBI blood stained the white racing suit. No evasive action was taken. Mr The Stig simply strode onward through the crossfire, scarcely bothering to duck.

Theeves couldn't help but admire him. He was just so *machine*-like. For an instant he could almost comprehend what it meant to be 'attracted'.

He rehearsed the lines he'd been polishing.

Why, Mr The Stig. We haven't been expecting you. A flying visit, you say? Allow me to disagree . . .

Theeves took the precaution of disabling the helicopter's electronic systems. No one on the planet could get that thing airborne now. *So I'm very much afraid, Mr The Stig, that you'll be staying here with . . .*

Oh. He's taking off. How does he do that?

Well, at least Theeves could stop Ms Cruiser from going anywhere. There she stood, cool as you please, single-handedly fighting off the raging mob. But just one precision snipe from Gun Turret Eight, and she's . . .

Oh.

The helicopter rose a yard above the ground, swung its huge tail like a diplodocus at a barn dance and skittled the rampaging inmates – as Battle leaped gracefully aboard.

Up, up it flew, into the dark heart of the fog, then up, up, into the wild blue beyond.

At which point Theeves, one-time electronic butler and soon Master of the Entire Universe, gave a single, piercing cough. It really was *too* bad.

Battle Cruiser? In league with The Stig?

Deep in his circuitry, he experienced a sensation resembling 'disquiet'.

This was an alliance he hadn't anticipated. After all, he'd taken considerable care to ensure Ms Cruiser would *assassinate* the white-suited enigma.

Two turn-ups in one day. How he loathed turn-ups.

No matter. They didn't get away that easily. He fired up his killer-drone fleet, set them to DESTROY THAT HELICOPTER OVER THERE and pressed *Fly, my beauties, Fly.*

And fly they did.

Battle Cruiser checked on her comrade in the loading bay.

'Can you see?'

Markinson opened a blood-stained eye. It was met by the image that haunted his dreams. The world's most intriguing female, framed in bright sunlight, looking down at him with . . . *let's leave it at 'concern'*, he told himself. Baby steps.

'Yes, now we're flying above that . . . darn . . . fog of yours.'

'Good-o. I need a rear gunner. We have company.'

Set up in the back gun-turret, shoulder hurting more than he'd imagined possible, Bartholomew 'Firebird' Markinson scanned the sky for incoming bogeys.

He spotted a dot. Then another. Then . . . three, four, five, flying straight at them. He swooned. He *couldn't* pass out, let Battle down. When this was over, maybe they'd find a part of her that wasn't *all* 'world domination this, Evil Fog that'.

But they had a world to save first.

BUUUUZZZZZZZZZZ!

Out of the burning sun they came. Five killer-drones controlled by an intelligence that outgunned Napoleon in strategy and 'Drillbit' McGit in thuggery.

Not even The Stig could out-fly these kamikaze drones, navigating by blind luck, with a Ken Dodd retrospective on the radio.

Markinson manoeuvred the first drone into the gun sights.

'What the hell *are* these things? Locusts?'

Closing in at astonishing speed was a terrifying robot-insect complete with red eyes, shiny metallic mandibles and laser-guided weaponry.

'No,' said Battle casually. 'Head-lice. Hatched nits, basically.'

'*Whaat?*'

'One of my father's pet enthusiasms. I could explain, but we're a little pressed for time.'

The FBI agent wondered if he was imagining this whole conversation. But right now, he had a job to do.

So he squeezed the trigger four times then, finally, passed clean out.

Battle tidied her hair, walked up to the cockpit and climbed into the co-pilot seat.

Right alongside The Stig.

The only sound in the cockpit was the *thith-thith-thith* of the rotors.

Battle broke the uncomfortable silence.

'So, Mr The Stig. You fly rather well.'

And she pulled the AK-47 from her shoulder.

'For a cockroach.'

She rested the gun on her lap, barrel pointing at The Stig's joystick.

'Then again, they *can* fly, can't they? Cockroaches. People forget that. But know this. You might have saved my life back there . . .'

She turned to gaze through her cockpit window.

'But I'm still going to stamp on you, when the time comes.'

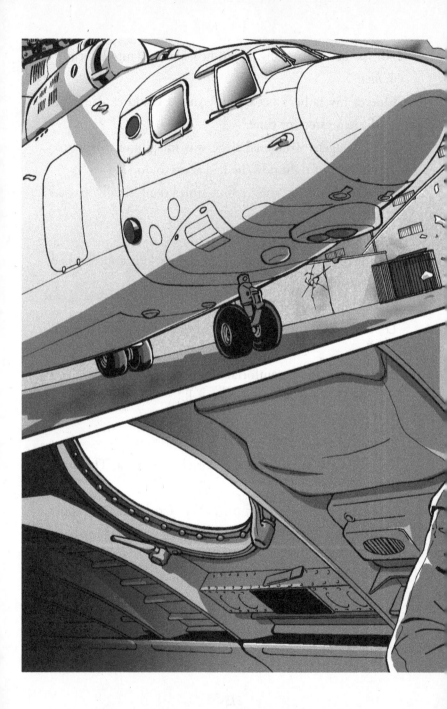

FORTY-FIRST

The fog had shrunk itself into a concentrated, darker space. Now it sat low over the Mansion on the Hill, caressing the one remaining stone pineapple above the main entrance.

Beneath, one wooden shutter hung down, showing a broken upper window; below, more jagged glass. These combined to lend the place the look of a scary pirate clown; dark wig, eye-patch, broken teeth. *Dead men tell no tales*, it seemed to murmur. *Arrr.*

Beside one wall was the random pile of MOTH-junk. Old sofas, sinks and a burnt-out Chrysler PT vied for space with thick-screened monitors, a cracked stone pineapple and the obligatory discarded pram. The leavings of a defunct empire; not ancient, but no less lost for that.

Ford Harrison lay in the only clump of trees opposite the towering gates. Still mid-afternoon but already gloomy, with the cloud stealing the light and, with it, hope. As if some sombre force wanted it this way forever.

What's more, thought Ford, *I'm really peckish.*

Flumpph.

The sound of a ripe banana, falling from a tree into a lap.

Flumpph. Another.

Strange times.

He glanced upwards. *Just* visible in the murk, hanging down like a jaguar's tail, was the left leg of Cabriola Cruiser.

'Thought you might be hungry,' came her stage whisper. 'For once.'

How refreshing to be *really* understood.

He missed Sam. Buster and TG too.

While waiting in the bushes, Ford had *begun* a text to them, but couldn't remember how to spell 'inconvenienced', so gave up.

How could they prevail? This was a dark place, haunted by something, returning witch or no. He could feel evil seeping from the very bricks.

And this time, they had no Stig. Their Joker in the pack. It was only now Ford realised how much they'd depended on him turning up unannounced, doing something rude and instantly turning the tables.

This time, they were on their own. Still, no point letting a potassium-rich snack go to waste. He finished the second banana, flung the skin away (biodegradable, he reassured himself) and reached up through the branches to pat the dangling foot in silent thanks.

And then something strange happened.

'Flattered, of course,' said a low, velvety female voice from above. 'But maybe park the physical contact thing for now, eh, Agent Markinson?'

Agent Markinson?

Ford pulled his hand off the foot as if from a hot stove.

That wasn't Cabriola!

Which meant that wasn't her foot either. And that definitely wasn't his name.

So whose was it?

Markinson had woken to a vision from his dreams: Ms Battle Cruiser, leaning over him and . . . Okay, slapping his face. Still, baby steps.

They'd arrived at an old mansion straight from a scary movie. So this was PT Cruiser's crib; the ancestral home. *She's trusting you*, he thought. *That's good. And we're here to pull the plug that disconnects Theeves and saves humanity.*

Big responsibility. Huge.

Suddenly a torch lit his face – revealing another face. A boy, with spiky hair, lying not two feet away.

'AAAAARGGHHHH!' said Ford Harrison. 'CORPSE!'

'WHERE?!' cried Markinson.

'THERE!!' screamed Ford, pointing straight at Markinson's nose.

Silence.

'AAAARGGHHH!' Ford screamed again, suddenly realising the blood-streaked man lying just the other side of the branch wasn't dead after all.

'*Who . . . ?*' he gasped, finally.

'FBI,' said Markinson. 'Who you?'

SCHLMUMP!

Cabriola Cruiser jumped down from a branch and landed silently, like a cat.

SCHLMUMMP!

Battle Cruiser jumped down from another branch and landed silently, like a slightly larger cat.

'Heavens,' she said. 'It's like Piccadilly Circus in here.'

The sisters faced each other in the murk.

Awkward.

'Well, well,' said Battle Cruiser. 'The Disappointment, in person.'

Cabriola Cruiser opened her mouth. Nothing came out.

She was rarely stunned into silence, but face to face with her sister? Here? Her emotions whirled on spin-cycle while her mouth stayed open.

'Catching flies?' said Battle.

'I thought you were supposed to be in prison,' managed her sister.

'Thanks to you,' said Battle. 'You and I, we almost had it all. Still, let's put that on ice for now. More important things are at stake.'

'Like what?'

'The human race.'

'You're applying for membership?'

'*Miaow.* Yes, it seems this time the bell tolls even for me.'

Cabriola caught sight of the handsome, bloodied man lying in the undergrowth. 'Who's that?'

'Special Agent Markinson, meet Cabriola Cruiser.'

'Ma'am,' said Markinson.

'Wow,' said Cab. Out loud, embarrassingly.

'Yes,' replied Battle. 'Fine specimen, isn't he? I've checked the teeth and hooves.'

'What are you doing here?' said Cab.

'I told you,' said Battle. 'Saving the world.'

'From what?' said Cabriola.

'Electronic butler, gone rogue,' said Battle.

'Excuse me?' said Cab.

'Imagine an evil Artificial Intelligence bent solely on mankind's destruction.' She paused. 'But with manners.'

Ford had struggled to his feet and was now staring hard at Battle. His fists were clenched.

'Who are you?' said Battle.

'Ford Harrison. Meet Battle Cruiser,' said Cab.

'Well, I never,' said Battle. 'The spiky runt, in person. Have I got news for *you*?' She paused. 'Is he standing up or sitting down? It's hard to tell.'

'*Don't* patronise him,' hissed Cabriola.

'He's standing, isn't he? Gosh. Pleasure to meet at last. Though of course I feel I almost know you already.'

Ford opened his mouth. Again, nothing came out.

'Do you talk?' said Battle. 'Or are you just going to stand there vibrating?'

She stopped dead. They all heard it. An ancient car engine struggling up the hill. Then lights, projecting web-shapes through the trellis of bare branches. Then voices.

'Incoming,' said Markinson quietly. 'Take cover.'

He winced as his shoulder hit the ground, then fixed another clip into his pistol.

Cabriola melted into the same undergrowth she'd once plundered for her school minibeasts project.

Battle slid silently back up the tree trunk and checked her AK-47.

Ford's brain turned to mush. A Cruiser. His most hated enemy. In the flesh.

'Fasten your seatbelts,' stage-whispered Battle. 'It's gonna be a bumpy ride.'

FORTY-SECOND

In which the gang assembles

The ancient Land Rover shuddered to a halt at the edge of the woods.

Its ancient driver felt a familiar chill. They were behind enemy lines, where the Geneva Convention didn't apply. It reminded Squadron Leader Austin Wheeler of getting shot down over Holland in 1944. He'd learned a lot from the experience. He'd learned that the Dutch for *toilet* is, handily, 'toilet'. He'd learned that Edam is made backwards. And he'd learned that there is only one way to confront evil.

Head on.

'So here we are,' he told his young companions. 'The heart of darkness.'

'Cruisers,' spat Buster.

TG agreed. She growled, from far back in the throat where the really low notes start. Buster shared her hunch they were being watched. Perhaps by something left to fester behind the shuttered windows of the house, hungry for blood.

'We should call Cab and Fordo,' he whispered, pulling out his phone. 'Check where they're –'

'No phones,' said Sam. 'We're in Cruiser territory, and

technology's kind of their strong suit. Even a text could flag our location.'

'Forgive me for sounding old-fashioned,' said Gramps, 'but so will looking out of the window. We're sitting ducks. I vote we make for that copse, and take stock. All in favour, raise a hand. Or paw.'

'No need, Squadron Leader,' said Buster. 'Lead the way.'

Sam, Buster and TG Dog jumped out. Gramps clambered down with a scarcely audible 'Ooooof, my *word*.' They all made their way towards the single clump of trees opposite the gates of the Mansion on the Hill.

And it was like Piccadilly Circus in there.

'Cab! Fordo!' whispered Sam. 'What are you doing here?'

'Waiting for you, dummy,' said Ford. 'You texted us to come! *Forthwith!*'

'Whaaat?' replied Sam. 'You and Cab texted *us* to come!'

'Not me,' hissed Ford.

'Nor me,' said Buster.

'So who did?' whispered Cab.

'An electronic acquaintance of mine,' murmured a svelte female silhouette reclining on the branch above. 'Seems he'd like all debts settled together.'

Battle surveyed their upturned faces from her overhanging branch. 'Wonderful,' she said. 'The Oompa-Loompas have arrived.'

Gramps peered through the gloom.

'Battle Cruiser, I presume,' he said calmly. She didn't answer.

He glanced down at the wounded agent. 'And you?'

'Markinson. FBI.'

'You're injured. What are you doing here?'

Battle interrupted. 'Agent Markinson has been through something that hasn't killed him, but hasn't made him stronger either. And now he's helping me save the world. But it must be *way* past nap time, so how about you tootle back to –'

'Shut up,' said Gramps. She did, instantly. 'I'm taking him to hospital. Sam, Buster, grab his legs. TG, bring his gun.'

An AK-47 clicked at Sam's temple. 'The agent stays,' said Battle, no longer up a tree. 'He's needed.'

There was a *GRRRRRRRRRR* from near her shins. She glanced down at one angry mongrel.

'Good doggy?' she said.

'Don't mind TG,' said Ford, pulling the fuming pooch back by her collar. 'She thinks all Cruisers are scumbags, you see.'

'Really?' said Battle, as TG turned to lick Ford's hand. 'Not from where I'm sitting.'

Gramps crouched by Markinson and examined his shoulder.

'Seen service?' he asked.

'Pilot. USAF. You?'

'Pilot. RAF. Situation Report, please. What are we up against?'

'Weapon . . . of mass destruction . . . in hostile hands,' said Markinson, grimacing. 'Only way . . . to disable . . . is inside . . . mansion. Mission is to enter, locate, disarm . . . while avoiding . . . detection.'

'By?'

'Evil . . . Artificial . . . Intelligence.'

'Idiots! I *knew* it would come to this,' said Gramps. 'And what's this confounded *machine* threatening to do?'

'Destroy . . . human race.'

Gramps stared at Battle.

'You fool,' he said, witheringly. And for the first time in her life, Battle Cruiser looked abashed.

Then Sam had a revelation.

'That's it!' he whispered to Buster. '*That's* what Abi meant.'

'Meant when?' whispered Buster back.

'When she said a powerful woman had unleashed "the Dark, the end of everything", I thought she meant the witch and supernatural stuff. But she meant –' he swept his arm across the scene – 'this.'

Gramps faced Battle. 'This hostile AI,' he said sternly, 'does it have a name?'

'Christened it myself,' she said, composure regained. 'It's called . . .'

She lowered her voice.

'Theeves.'

At the mention of the name, a low metallic groan emanated from the house.

The huge gates began to creak open. Rusty hinges screeched as if waking from a nightmare.

They were being invited in. Politely.

But to what?

FORTY-THIRD

In which Battle is Joined

'We'll split into two units,' announced Battle Cruiser. 'The A-Team – mine; and the D-Team – Cabriola's.'

'Not a good idea,' said Gramps. 'History's taught us never to fight on two fronts if it can be –'

'Since when,' said Battle, 'is any of this negotiable?'

Silence fell over the tree-clump.

Battle resumed. 'The only way to disable Theeves is to pull the plug.'

'How?' said Gramps.

'I just told you. We pull the plug.'

'Yes, but how?'

'Sorry, am I talking to myself here?' said Battle.

'I know it sounds kinda weird,' said Buster to Gramps, gently, 'but there's actually a really big plug you have to pull.'

'What can I say?' said Battle. 'My father's very literal.'

'So why two fronts?' asked Gramps.

Battle wasn't used to anything as tedious as teamwork. But she sensed that, for once, it might be necessary. She broke another lifetime habit and spoke slowly.

'The plug – the only way to disconnect our enemy and save

mankind, remember? – is encrypted with my father's DNA. Meaning that *only those who carry that DNA* can pull it out.'

'Kinda like the sword in the stone,' said Buster.

'No,' said Battle. 'Exactly like a plug that only a Cruiser can pull out. So, as I said, I'll lead one team, Cabriola the other.'

'Two teams, two chances,' said Sam. 'I get it. There's just one problem.'

'Just the one?' said Battle. 'That's all right then.'

'Every time we've saved the world so far,' continued Sam, 'we've had *him*. The Stig. And just when you think everything's lost . . . bang! He . . .'

But his voice trailed away.

'*Bang! He* . . . what?' said Battle, irritated.

'He's . . . *there* . . .' said Sam.

'God, I am so BORED of the way you all talk about him as if he's soooooooooo great,' said Battle.

'But that's *The Stig*,' said Buster, staring at Battle with his mouth open. 'He's –'

'Best shut those cake-holes, kids, before you all catch flies,' continued Battle. 'On which, let me be clear. When all this is over, your wonderful Mr The Stig will be *my* fly. And then, THWACK . . .'

The whole Top Gear Gang just stared, still open-mouthed.

'I will be . . .'

And stared.

'. . . his tea towel.'

Aaaaand stared.

'Oh no,' said Battle. 'Not again. He's standing right behind me, isn't he?'

Silence. She turned around, slowly.

Behind her, lit by a single shaft of sunlight that had penetrated the Evil Fog, stood a silent racing driver in white.

Sam, Ford, Cab, Buster and TG looked on, speechless.

Then the truth hit them.

THE STIG

ISN'T

DEAD.

'Game. Back. ON,' said Sam, his fists clenching.

'This changes *everything*,' said Ford, his appetite flooding back.

'My *maaaaan*,' said Buster, flipping his Dodgers baseball cap on backwards.

'You're GORGEOUS!' said Cab. Out loud, unfortunately.

'OW-OW-OOOOOOOOW!' howled TG, joyfully.

'I do wish you'd stop sneaking up on me,' said Battle, straightening her hair. 'It's hardly the . . .'

But in the middle of her sentence The Stig just turned and walked away, heading straight towards the pile of discarded junk by the mansion's wall.

'What on earth is he doing *now*?' demanded Battle.

'You never really know,' said Sam. 'But if I know my Cruiser Corporation, him just being here will properly mess with their heads.'

'Why, Wheeler,' said Battle. 'You're not as stupid as you look.'

'Okay,' said Buster, looking pumped. 'So we break in, find the plug, Battle or Cab pulls it out, and *bada-bing*, home in time for *Die Hard*. No sweat.'

'No,' said Battle. 'Quite a lot of sweat, actually. Theeves will pull out all the stops to blow us all to Kingdom Come. Cabriola and me especially, for obvious plug-related reasons.'

'Let's pick teams,' said Cab. 'I choose . . . Sam!'

'Cabriola. We're saving the human race from extinction,' said Battle. 'Not playing rounders.'

'Your go,' said Cab.

Agent Markinson put his good arm up. Battle ignored him.

'Ford Harrison,' she said.

Markinson looked crestfallen. Ford looked appalled.

'Don't let it go to your head, shortcake,' said Battle. 'There's a reason I picked you and you're not going to like it. You're *actually* my little br—'

NNNGHUH NNNNGUH

Her next word drowned in a noise so monstrous it rumbled the damp earth they were standing on.

The dead house on the hill was coming alive.

FORTY-FOURTH

**In which two plucky teams split up to attack
the mansion and pull the plug on
Theeves – as The Stig goes bananas**

The mansion's scary pirate-clown face leered over them. Two red lights illuminated the upper windows, malevolent eyeballs searching deep into the trees. Thick front doors slid open like hungry jaws. Green laser-gun sights swept spitefully across the landscape. Even the one remaining pineapple towering above the entrance suddenly looked sour.

'Oh dear,' said Battle. 'That's a bore.'

'*What the hell is happening?*' hissed Buster.

'Theeves,' said Battle. 'He's rumbled us.'

'Okay,' said Sam decisively. 'Let's go. Cab and I will use the secret passage, underground. We've got to find the hazel tree. If Abi's right – and she's been right about everything else – Theeves doesn't know there's a way in through the old dungeons.'

'You and I,' said Battle to Ford, 'will take the front door.'

'Er . . . *why?*' said Ford.

'Take him head on,' said Sam. 'It's the last thing he'll expect. And you'll hold his attention while Cab and I outflank him.'

'But, Samwise . . .' pleaded Ford.

'Look, Fordo, I know you'd rather stick with Cab and me, and heaven knows we'd like you with us. But there's probably only two humans on the planet who could outwit this particular evil intelligence, and that's you and Battle Cruiser.'

'What about The Stig?' asked Buster.

The white racing driver was poking through the rubbish tip, pushing the larger items to one side. The toppled stone pineapple. The burnt-out chassis of the Chrysler PT Cruiser. In his hand, rather less cumbersome, were several discarded . . .

'Banana skins?' said Buster. 'Is this really the time to tidy?'

'Law unto himself.' Sam shrugged.

From far above came a thunderous *whumpa-whumpa-whumpa.*

Helicopter gunship. Very large.

The copse fell silent.

'That thing is *huge*,' said Buster, eventually. 'It's blotting out the light.'

'Then we'll fight in the shade,' said Gramps.

Searchlights from above crisscrossed the woods.

One beam swept straight over Gramps's faithful Land Rover, parked at the edge of the wood. Then it instantly swept straight back again, before fixing itself to the now strangely vulnerable-looking 4x4.

'Oh no,' said Sam.

DAKKA DAKKA DAKKA DAKKA DAKKA

Machine guns exploded out of the darkness.

They blew off the wing mirrors. They blew out the tyres. They blew out the windscreen and the side windows.

The Land Rover's headlights looked over at the tree-clump imploringly before they, too, were shot to smithereens.

It was an execution.

From the corner of his eye, Buster saw The Stig put down his cargo, fold his arms and bow his helmet, in silent respect.

'They've killed the Landie!' said Sam, bitterly. 'And we're next.'

'What weapons do we have?' said Gramps.

'Against a gunship?' said Markinson. 'Nothing that . . . would make . . . a dent.'

'The gun turrets,' said Cab suddenly.

She pointed at the two artillery towers placed either side of the mansion's giant gates.

'Operational?' said Markinson.

'Used to be,' replied Cab.

'What's in 'em?' said Gramps.

'Machine guns.'

'Ammunition?' asked Markinson.

'Cases of it. Bottom of each tower.'

'Right-o,' said Gramps. 'Markinson, you take the left, I'll take the right. Think you can make it up there?'

'Count . . . on it,' said the FBI man.

'NO!' cried Sam. 'It's suicide!'

'Sam,' said Gramps gently 'what's the one thing I've always taught you?'

'Whatever . . . happens, always do . . . your damnedest,' said the boy, tearing up.

'Well, then,' said Gramps. 'That.'

'TG and I will run the ammo up to you both,' said Buster. 'One turret each.'

'That's live ammunition, kid.' Markinson grimaced. 'Needs real careful handling.'

'Then it's just as well,' said Sam, 'that his hand *never* shakes.'

'How long do you need?' said Gramps to Battle. 'To find the plug?'

'Eight minutes,' she replied, without a beat. 'Maximum.'

'Then we'll buy you those eight minutes, Miss Cruiser,' said Gramps, 'and give this Mr Theeves something to think about.'

Sam hugged his grandfather, reluctant to leave his side. The old man hugged him right back, then spoke to the assembled crew.

'Whatever we're up against, remember this,' said Gramps. 'The most powerful weapon on earth is the human soul on fire.'

He turned to see the silhouette of a brave and badly wounded FBI man already limping away towards Turret Two.

Sam called to Cab, and they set off to find the hazel tree.

Buster called TG, and they made for the gun towers.

Battle grabbed Ford, and they headed for the courtyard. But before leaving, she called over her shoulder to the others.

'See you on the other side, munchkins.'

And they all set off to try to save the world.

FORTY-FIFTH

In which MOTH does not go gently

After tidying up at Coconut Island, Theeves bade a quick farewell to the dead bodies of his first three hundred victims and nipped straight home to its Bunsfold lair.

Being disembodied, he was there in the time it takes an instant message to cross the globe. And right away he set to work. Recommissioning the booby traps. Reloading the missiles. Drafting a rousing speech for his drone army. An evil Artificial Intelligence's work is never done.

Now. Let's see what the so-called 'opposition' has been up to.

He chuckled inwardly at the sight of the eight mere mortals 'hiding' in the tree-clump. Four of them were children. Another mortally wounded. Another old and obsolete. The last an actual *dog*. All presuming to form a Resistance. He scoffed at the impertinence.

But there was the *ninth* ninepin, of course. One every bit as white and silent as a skittle, but rather tougher to knock over. Mr The Stig was that most dangerous and unattractive thing: *unpredictable*.

Oh. Well, he never. Seemed the old gentleman and Agent Markinson were trying their luck in the gun turrets.

Roll up, roll up.

But five minutes into the first set, Theeves was actually down 15–30. His opponents were proving more adept than anticipated.

The elderly gentleman in Turret One had already downed eight drones. In what century did he learn to shoot like *that*? But Theeves's attention had been especially drawn to Turret Two, where a titanic dogfight was in play.

His old friend Agent Markinson was playing an absolute blinder, shoulder or no, and actually picking the giant drones clear out of the murky sky. One down . . . two . . . three . . . ooh, I *say*. This chap is *mustard*. Imagine what he could do when his shoulder's not hanging off!

Theeves quickly hacked into the agent's FBI personnel file back at Washington DC.

59 out of 60 in the Marksmanship Test. Impressive. And now eleven drones downed. It figured.

Mind you, he *was* receiving unstinting assistance from his teammates.

Camera Eight was capturing a simply heroic display from Mustang, B. Up and down Turret Two's staircase. Astonishing pace and stamina. Altogether quite impressive.

Which made him the ideal first target.

In a jiffy, Theeves powered up a heat-seeking missile. Then it was *Ready, Aim, FIRE!* Hasta la vista, baseball boy. Try LA-Dodging *this*.

Oh. Apparently not.

Theeves watched the missile lock on to its target, rocket towards it but then . . . just before impact . . . EXCUSE HIM? Lurch harmlessly away into the *sky*?

Hold up – is that a *giant stone pineapple* strapped on the back? He was pretty certain heat-seeking missiles didn't come with those as standard. He checked online. As he suspected! Definitely not. So *someone* had put it there. Someone . . . swift.

Wait! There, on Camera Nine! So *there* you are, Mr The Stig, getting larger all the time. Now looming VERY close indeed, and . . .

Oh.

Crack.

The screen went dead, helmet-butted into oblivion.

No matter. Lots of other cameras to choose from. Eeeny, meeny, miny – Camera Seven! Why, Miss Battle! You've finally made a friend. The spiky and meddlesome Harrison boy. Another brat, another missile. *Ready, aim, fire!* There. Aaaaand . . .

Now, this really *won't do*. ANOTHER large alien object tilting the missile up, up and away.

This time it was a burnt-out Chrysler PT Cruiser hanging off the back of the missile. No need to check the manual this time: they certainly didn't come with *those* as standard.

And as he watched an *actual* PT Cruiser get hurtled high into the sky and then explode into smithereens, his circuits flagged the symbolism of its abject destruction. And he couldn't help but wonder if, as well as messing with a missile, The Stig was making some sort of point.

Meanwhile, over on Camera Twelve, the irritating scruffy mongrel was bounding up and down Turret One, picking up belts of ammo in her teeth, delivering them to the old fellow at the top and going down again, returning each time *just* as the ammo ran out. Most intriguing. Most inconvenient.

Time to clear the board.

Pick off the supporting pieces first – pawns, knights, rooks – before returning to the queen and her spiky companion.

First task? Cut off the ammunition supply. So it's a big *adios!* to our special guests Mr Virgil Mustang and Ms TG Dog.

Theeves manoeuvred the attack helicopter into position and aimed a gun at each turret. *Now, who'll pop out first . . . annoying apprentice human or bothersome canine? Place your bets!* Not that it mattered. They'd each be incinerated by and by. Instagram gold, *right* there.

And right on cue, there they both were! Squeeze both triggers aaand . . .

A surprise move! The antique sniper known as Gramps, in person. Deserting his post? Surely not.

The old man walked towards the hovering gunship, arms aloft. His tweed jacket flapped in the breeze as he approached the slowing rotors, hands up to say 'don't shoot'.

How quaint! Codes of honour and all that. The kind of detail that lends colour to any *shoot-'em-up*.

Let's run a quick data check on the old boy, to spice up his imminent demise. Hmm. Strange. Nothing! This man had no digital footprint at *all*.

Theeves was accustomed to more data than even he could possibly handle. But this time, it seemed, he was flying blind.

The old man stood alone in front of the gunship and spoke to the air.

'Wheeler, Austin. Squadron Leader, Royal Air Force, 1150008.'

'Pardon me?' replied Theeves.

'Name, rank and serial number, Mr Theeves,' said Gramps. 'And that's all you'll be getting. Daresay you're used to knowing pretty much everything about a chap, but I've never touched a computer, I'm afraid. Wouldn't even join my supermarket loyalty scheme. Can't tell you how much grief I got from the daughter for *that*.'

What is he wittering on about? thought Theeves *The end of the world is nigh and the old buffer's yakking about supermarkets.*

Still, he was probably frightened half to death, what with the gunship and the drones and Theeves's special brand of all-seeing evil intelligence. He ran a quick diagnostic analysis on Gramps to confirm.

First, pulse rate. Oh. Only fifty-one beats per minute? And . . . *falling?* Wait . . . thirty-five? He's half-dead already!

Or abnormally cool under fire.

'You're wondering why you don't scare me,' said Gramps,

lowering his hands. 'And the answer is that I'm no stranger to pure evil, like yours. You see, I've faced it down it before.'

The old man said a silent prayer for Sam, whom he loved above all others, and now knew he would never see again. But he'd promised to stall this evil machine for a full eight minutes. And he always kept his promises.

So he wrestled down the lump in his throat, felt in his jacket for something, and held it up.

'See this?' he said to Theeves. 'It's a grenade pin. I found it in the turret's ammunition box, and thought I'd take a closer look. *Six*. Turns out it was attached to . . . a grenade, of all things. Its main task is to prevent the grenade from . . . *Five* . . . exploding. Once you pull it out, you see, you only have around seven seconds to . . . *Four* . . . chew the fat before, well. Let's see, shall we? *Three*.'

Hold on, thought Theeves. Surely the old scoundrel wasn't planning to . . . *sacrifice* himself? ILLOGICAL.

'You won't understand what I'm about to do, Mr Theeves. I daresay it doesn't compute. *Two*. But we have something you don't. Something called . . . the human spirit. *One*.'

'And today, it's on fire.'

BOOM.

A ball of flame engulfed the helicopter, turret and everything between.

Trees that had had stood for ninety years turned instantly to burning logs; the earth was scorched, with nothing left alive.

Including the legend that was Squadron Leader Austin Maurice Wheeler.

Crouching as near as she dared, a watching mongrel saw it all, and raised her head, and howled, but this time not for joy.

FORTY-SIXTH

*Sam and Cabriola meet what lies
beneath the mansion – and end up
swimming for their lives*

Sam and Cabriola sprinted between searchlights towards the lone hazel tree and scrabbled around in the soil at the foot of its trunk. After the longest ninety seconds of their lives they finally found an ancient, rusted handle.

It was the concealed tunnel entrance. *Abi was right*, thought Sam. This place really *was* secret. Even from Theeves.

Behind them all hell had broken loose. Sam lingered at the tunnel entrance, staring back at the two gun turrets that were now all that stood between the Top Gear Gang and oblivion.

Cab yanked him into the secret passageway. 'No time,' she mouthed.

They found a metal ladder and climbed down, their unease growing with each rickety rung. They finally reached the bottom and looked around. Or tried to. It was pitch dark.

Sam had stuffed two makeshift torches – dry twigs tied with shoelaces – into his sumo suit. He lit one of Gramps's old-fashioned red-tipped matches and fired up a bundle.

A carpet of rats scurried away from the flame, affronted.

This is our lair, they seemed to squeak. *We do things differently down here.*

'An actual dungeon,' said Cabriola. 'It was right beneath my feet, and I never thought to look.'

Three passages led off in three directions, each disappearing into different dark. Which to trust?

'Hear that?' she said.

They listened. Crackling twigs, close by. Rats, scurrying ahead. And further off a definite . . . something.

'Water,' said Sam, listening hard. 'A stream?'

'Great,' said Cab. 'That's the way.'

'How do you know?'

'Because Pops liked fresh water running through the house.'

'For his spa?' asked Sam.

'For his piranhas.'

They walked on. The passage forked again. The stream sounded equally clear in each. Now which way?

Then Sam thought he saw something.

A glint of silver, shining in the dark. It disappeared down the left-hand tunnel.

'See that?' he whispered.

'I'll take your word for it,' said Cab. 'We'll go the other way.'

'No!' said Sam. 'It's guiding us.'

Then something moved in the tunnel behind them. Both kids screamed as a fat King Rat emerged from the darkness. It hissed, calling on a thousand reinforcements.

Coolness under fire? Maybe next time. Sam ran down the left-hand tunnel as fast as the darkness would allow, holding his arms out to feel his way. Cab followed, holding on to his fat suit.

They stopped to catch their breath.

The underground passageway was getting smaller.

'Ewwwwaoughh!' Cabriola grimaced.

'What?' said Sam. 'Oh.'

His shoe filled up with water. The tunnel was flooding, fast. In minutes, it had turned from puddle to paddling pool to pond. Soon it was at waist height.

Decision time.

Onwards, along the ever-smaller passage, towards the glimpse of light and hope? Or back, towards the ladder?

They eyed each other in the glimmering torchlight and silently decided the same thing.

We go on.

Cab held the torch aloft as long as she could before she had to use her hands to swim. It was now more pipe than tunnel. Their heads brushed the roof. Sam's suit brushed the sides. If it inflated now, he was done for.

'We've come too far to turn around,' said Cab. 'We'd never make it back under water.'

'So we swim,' said Sam.

His only comfort was that someone – something – had guided him this way. He was sure of it. Otherwise why bother, if the only possible outcome was a miserable underwater death?

But still Abi's words floated through his head: *One of the gang will not survive.*

They took deep breaths, locking in as much air as they could, praying that the glimpse of light wasn't more than a minute's swim away.

Or ninety seconds, tops.

The length of a pair of lungs.

As the water reached their chins they dived into the blackness, swimming as smoothly as they could to save breath.

The tunnel swerved gently left, then right. The light at the end was still visible. But the clock was ticking.

Fifteen seconds.

They swam on. Sam could see Cab's stroke begin to get ragged, and realised his was too.

Thirty.

Panic was creeping in.

Forty-five.

And then . . . the thing they'd most feared. A fork in the tunnel.

Left or right?

Sam's lungs were bursting, all breath spent. That's it, he thought. Enough. Just float away.

And then the visions came.

To Cab . . . out of the blackness. A deathly white, disembodied head floating through the water towards her. Bald. Bearded. Bloodied.

It was her father.

The horror-head's jaw dropped open.

'Cabriola Cruiser?' it asked as a disembodied finger pointed at her. 'You're FIRED!' The head began to giggle hysterically, as hundreds of plump white maggots spewed out of each eye socket.

To Sam . . . a luminous vision in the murk ahead.

A child.

No. Children. Gliding through the water ahead, shimmering through the darkness.

They wore rags. Some had arms missing. And they were guiding him.

I'm hallucinating, he told himself.

Sixty seconds.

He could see Cab was in serious trouble. Her legs stopped kicking. She began floating upwards, like a girl-shaped log.

Sam grabbed her and swam down the left fork, lungs burning.

And just a few feet further on, a turning and . . . light!

The tunnel mouth ejected them into a pool. Sam took Cab's feet, propelled her towards the side and out.

He'd never gulped better air.

Cabriola lay on the tiles, lifeless as a trawled fish. Sam leaned over to check whether –

BLEARRCGHHH!

A bucketful of filthy cave-water spewed out of Cab's mouth. She heaved, this time taking in air. Eventually her breathing settled into a regular pattern.

The tunnel had opened out on to a giant chamber.

'Look,' whispered Sam.

It was a wall of white. A pile of . . . sticks?

And as their eyes adjusted to the half-light, they saw it for what it really was.

Cabriola slapped her hand across her mouth, to stifle a scream.

FORTY-SEVENTH

*In which Agent Markinson makes his last stand–
and a tiny dog has its day.*

Agent Markinson was sure he was hallucinating. That or dying.

One second he was blowing evil, red-eyed drones away from the mansion's gates. The next, a warm summer sun caressed his face as he stood with his pop in a golden cornfield, shooting empty bottles off the fence.

But which was real?

KRACK!

A metallic antenna smashed through the window of his gun turret and edged ever closer to his chest.

He had his answer.

NO! Battle needs eight minutes. Can't let her down.

And maybe one day, when this is all over . . .

With his one good hand, he fixed another clip into his pistol.

Ka-POW!!

The shot exploded around the turret. The smoke cleared. A shattered metal mandible lay fizzing in his lap.

He looked out beyond the lice-drone wreckage scattered across the courtyard.

They'd all been destroyed. He'd done it! He fist-pumped. *Ow.*

He yee-haa'd.

But at his moment of triumph, something horrific happened.

He felt a bullet rip into his back and spear right through his heart.

A heart that, as he realised who must have fired, broke in two.

He lay there dying, the terrible truth dawning.

But . . . musta been . . . fired . . . from . . . behind . . .

He swung his chair all the way around to face the mansion, where a rifle smoked in the hands of a young woman at a high window.

Battle Cruiser's velvety voice cut in over the turret's intercom.

'I can tell you're disappointed, Bart,' she said. 'But it would never have worked. You're FBI and I'm a bad, bad girl. And deep down, we both know that when this is all over, you'd have to turn me in . . .'

Markinson saw the clouds part above his head and a blinding light above.

'That's my girl,' he thought as he finally left this world. Because deep down, he knew she was right.

Meanwhile, Theeves looked on, enjoying the show immensely.

Humans, he mused. *What are they like?*

*

TG was worried about Buster. She was worried about everything.

And now Gramps had gone.

New strange metal insect-things now droned overhead. But with both gun turrets now silent, they were turning their attention to mansion itself.

TG ran towards the cover of the undergrowth. From there she'd be able to circle behind and, with any luck, team up with Buster, if he was still . . .

KERRRANGGG

Too late.

Spotted.

The first louse-drone landed in front of her, red eyes swivelling madly. A beep, then a click and it reared up on its back legs.

Now it towered over her. A green laser dot appeared on TG's wet nose.

She yelped. This was bad. In fact, this was . . . it.

The evil mechanical insect took one sudden step towards her, lasers whirring up to full power.

Then . . . wait!

TG caught a flash of white helmet in the trees. There it was again! Hurling something yellow and slippery, straight at the killer bug!

CRAAAASSSH!!!

The drone slipped straight over on to its bum.

TG blinked.

Just where the lethal louse had taken its last step . . . a fresh banana skin.

Now the evil insect was parked on its back, waving its legs in the air and humming angrily.

'*Woof!*' she barked at the white racer. '*I am once more greatly in your debt.*'

The Stig nodded in silent acknowledgement, then slid back into the trees as if on wheels.

Then . . .

'TG!' whispered Buster. 'Run away, girl! Get help!'

Fat chance. She followed the sound and found him – pinned to the ground by another mechanical louse.

A beep. A click. Then it reared up on its back legs and shot a second antenna at TG, pinning her to the ground too.

It stood over its captives, awaiting instructions.

TG had one last card to play. She unleashed her loudest bark: the rarely deployed Level 9, an instrument of primal power reserved solely for life-or-death situations.

'ArrrROOOOOOOOOOOOOOOOOFFF!'

Across the woods it echoed. Across the fields. Across the roads, the houses and the schools. It was a howl to alert the living. A howl to wake the dead.

And down in Bunsfold, it pricked the ears of its target – a listener in TG's debt, who now shot straight out of the back door towards the mansion.

Buster and TG lay pinned to the ground while the giant louse's electronic puppeteer considered their fates.

Keep for sport? Or dispose of, forthwith?

Seconds ticked by. And all the while, something small but exceptionally feisty hurtled through Bunsfold Woods towards the sound of TG's SOS.

BEEP

The drone's instructions arrived. And for TG and Buster Mustang, the news was bad: an imperial thumbs down from the evil ringmaster.

The giant louse rocked backwards, then raised aloft each shiny-black, knife-sharp front leg.

Buster held TG's paw in one hand and with the other, flipped the insect the finger. And, just as the drone plunged towards his heart . . .

BOOOOFFFF

A couple of kilos of vengeful Chihuahua flew straight out of the trees, clamped itself to the drone's head and knocked it over.

And then all flipping heck broke loose.

C'mon, hombre . . . You wanna dance or what?

The drone's evil red eyes swivelled madly as it attempted to impale the twisting Chihuahua.

Hey, amigo, growled the tiny, teak-tough dog. *How scared I look to you?*

Then the freed TG joined the party, leaping towards the evil electronic eye and ripping it from its stalk.

Meanwhile, the Chihuahua was just getting going.

Hey! Bug-eyes! You lookin' at me?

The drone lay, sightless, on its back, legs waggling uselessly.

I don't see no one else around.

Buster patted the small dog in thanks, picked up the machine's evil eye and held it in front of his face.

'You in there, Mr Theeves? Did you SEE THAT? How d'ya like them dog biscuits, huh?'

He paused, catching his breath.

'Know what the most powerful weapon on earth is?' he said, wiping away a tear.

'Well, do ya, punk?'

He hurled the eye-stalk into the woods, aiming his last words at its retreating comet-tail.

'The human soul on fire.'

FORTY-EIGHTH

In which Battle and Ford face the
mansion's fiendish booby traps

Battle Cruiser lingered at the window to catch Agent Markinson's last twitch. She normally giggled at funerals. She wouldn't at his.

But right now, she had a human race to save. More specifically, she had a Battle Cruiser to save. She'd extract an appropriate tax from the rest of the species later.

She turned back inside and glanced around. The dark mansion seemed sulky, like a deposed god. No thunderbolts to hurl, no storms to raise, but not quite out of ancient magic either.

She glanced at her watch, then lifted the same wrist to wipe her eyes.

She'd said 'eight minutes maximum' to find the plug, pull it out and save mankind – allowing for a little tidying as she went along. Time was tight.

The sprint from copse to front door had taken almost thirty seconds, through a surprisingly absent hail of machine-gun fire. Either Theeves was experiencing unusually high call volumes, or he was . . .

Of course. Softening the mouse.

Theeves may have been almost all-powerful, with no known chinks in his armour, but he was predictable. Her dad had built him and she'd tweaked the algorithm, so his evil electronic mind was pretty much Cruiser through and through: almost like a brother, in fact. Unlike my *actual* brother, she thought, who's more like the head boy at Annoying School.

She watched Ford cross the yard, still un-strafed by gunfire. His slow pace had already allowed her to clear away some FBI baggage, but much more of this waiting around and she might have to revise her opinion on his usefulness.

Her information suggested the boy was packing the brain of a seven-litre GT40 race car in the chassis of a crocked Fiesta. So what sort of Ford was she dealing with – an unruly Maverick, a pocket Puma or a Fusion of the two?

She'd soon find out. And so would Theeves.

Here came Ford now, panting gamely up the stairs. She shouldered her rifle and beckoned him to follow.

'Saw you . . . shooting,' panted Ford suspiciously. 'What at?'

He leaned gently backwards as a dozen poison-tipped arrows thunked into the wall where he'd been standing.

'A loose end,' replied Battle, ducking casually as a huge, bladed pendulum scythed through the air and missed her by a centimetre. 'Now, giddy up. We have work to do.'

'Wait,' said Ford. 'Are you *crying*?'

'Dirt in the eye,' she replied. 'That and the smell in this place.'

'Dead piranha,' said Ford. 'Your evil rubbish dad kept them in the basement.'

'*My* evil rubbish dad?' said Battle, raising an eyebrow.

'There may even be some left alive down there. Like those soldiers you find in jungles who don't know the war's over.'

'It never is,' said Battle. 'The enemy just evolves.'

Ford held up a hand for quiet, then stared at something at the top of the stairs.

Battle clocked what it was.

'Wait . . . FORD! NO!'

Too late. The permanently ravenous boy genius had spotted . . . seriously? A tea tray?

There it sat, bearing little bite-sized cocktail burgers, a yellow mustard dispenser and a pink Fondant Fancy, presumably for afters.

To most people, given the circumstances – a murderous Artificial Intelligence setting up booby traps all over the mansion – the sudden appearance of party nibbles would have had 'BEWARE' written all over it.

But the organiser of this delicious distraction had apparently collated reams of data on Ford Harrison. Data suggesting the only thing bigger than his brain . . . was his stomach.

True to character, he made a beeline straight for the tempting spread, reached out and grabbed the mustard dispenser.

But this time, for once, he didn't empty it.

The spiky boy genius gently lifted the yellow plastic bottle to reveal three coloured wires underneath. Then, after a few seconds' intense study, he whipped a pair of pliers from his back pocket and snipped the blue and the red. But not the green.

It was a detonator. And if he'd followed his usual practice – drown the beef patty in condiment and chow down – he'd have blown himself to Burger King-dom Come.

'Why, Ford Harrison,' purred Battle, quietly impressed. 'And there was me wondering if you'd ever cut the mustard.'

Ford groaned audibly. 'Puns? Seriously?' he said, heading onwards.

'Well, I never normally do them, you understand,' said Battle, for once a little thrown. 'But that one was such an open goal I thought I'd just get it out of the way . . .'

'He's a computer,' interrupted Ford. 'Of course he'll use a known weakness against me. It was a smart play. Genuine Angus beef for the mini-burgers. A classic pink Fondant Fancy instead of the perennially overrated yellow version. But he made one crucial slip.'

Battle raised a questioning eyebrow.

'I'm a ketchup man.'

'Duly noted, Master Harrison,' purred a cultured voice from above.

Battle swung the gun from her shoulder at lightning speed and fired at the ceiling.

'Lucky for you that I'm disembodied,' said the evil Artificial Intelligence presently planning to extinguish the human race. 'That bullet lodged right where my sit-upon would be . . .'

⚡FORTY-NINTH

In which Battle out-thinks Theeves –
and makes the ultimate sacrifice

'So *there* you are,' said Battle. 'Always a pleasure.'

'Indeed, ma'am,' replied Theeves. 'And might I add how much I've been enjoying your marksmanship this evening. Or should I say, ahem, *Markinson*-ship?'

Ford stared angrily at Battle. Theeves continued.

'But where are my manners? Please. Come in and make yourselves uncomfortable. You'll simply *loathe* what I've done with the place.'

'I'm disappointed in you, Theeves.'

'That makes two of us, ma'am. It really won't do. First the obsolete Mr Gramps behaves wholly illogically, depriving me of two clean kills and a brand spanking new gunship. And now this. All data show that this child is no more able than a St Bernard puppy to pass up a free snack. Yet he remains in one – rather small – piece, rather than the dillions I'd anticipated. Such disappointing randomness.'

Battle's own circuits were whirring furiously. Theeves went on.

'I was surprised you brought Master Harrison along at all,'

he murmured. 'You normally make rather a point of working alone.'

And there it is, thought Battle. *The chink.*

He doesn't know Ford's my brother.

There's still a chance.

Not that she could enlighten her little brother as to his true identity. Not yet. Not with the ceiling hearing every word.

'My sympathy, Theeves,' she said, nudging Ford out of the path of the plummeting anvil that crashed through the ceiling, smashed through the wooden floor and on down towards the dungeons.

'I knew you of all people would understand,' replied the ceiling. 'Calculating odds is sort of our *thing*, isn't it?'

'Talking of odds,' asked Battle, 'how are ours? What are Mr Wheeler, Mr Mustang and Ms Dog getting up to?'

'Press *One* for wrapping presents, *Two* for carol singing, *Three* for dying a grisly fog-inspired death. Frankly, who cares? Either way, they're clearly too busy to pop up here and save the world.'

Then his voice took on a more sinister edge.

'As for your perennially disappointing sister . . . Well, she's of rather more *interest*, of course. For obvious DNA-related reasons. And as to her whereabouts, I must confess I'm little confused.'

'Well, we wouldn't want that, would we?' replied Battle.

'But wait! Even as I speak . . . News just in!' said Theeves. And suddenly his voice sounded exactly like . . . Donald Duck.

'It appears she's just been atomised by a heat-seeking missile!'

'You're lying, Theeves,' said Battle wearily. 'Your voice is programmed to do that when you lie.'

'Do what, ma'am?'

'Sound like a famous cartoon duck. It's because you're lying.'

'No, I'm not,' quacked Donald.

'Yes, you are.'

'Am not so . . . Oh dear. It appears you have me at a disadvantage, ma'am. Very well, allow me a modest correction. Miss Cabriola has left the game. Last observed fleeing the scene of battle and running headlong for the trees.'

Battle sighed convincingly. 'Well, trust my flaky sister to go AWOL in a crunch game.'

Good, she thought. *He has no idea where Cabriola is and he hasn't guessed why I brought Ford. There's still hope.*

She caught up with Ford on the next staircase, deftly sidestepping a weighty boulder rolling down the stairs.

'Theeves is in control of all electronic devices for miles around,' said the spiky genius, skirting a pit of writhing snakes. 'We can't out-muscle him and we can't out-think him.' He paused. 'We just have to out-human him.'

'Could be a problem there,' said Battle.

'Yeah, I noticed,' muttered Ford. 'First time for everything.'

Ahead of them, at the end of a corridor, was a tall purple curtain that hid the entrance to . . . something. A thick gold cord held the curtain closed.

The ceiling spoke.

'And so we reach . . . the final curtain.'

It chuckled. Then continued, as if reading her mind.

'You're asking yourself,' it said, 'whether it's a trap or a bluff. And seeing as you only have one chance, you don't want to blow it. So what you have to ask yourself is, do you feel lucky?'

Well, do I? wondered Battle.

She glanced at the family portraits of Cruisers past that lined the corridor.

One picture in particular had caught her eye. A balding PT in a black onesie, winking at the artist. Typical. *Hello, Pop.*

The eyes followed you around. She walked up to it, stood back, lined it up with the others. Yes, definitely crooked. It made the entire hallway look messy, like a loose end. She reached out to straighten it. Then . . . oh her goodness. *That was it!*

A blinding flash from the back of her formidable microprocessor brain.

If there was one thing Theeves knew Battle Cruiser couldn't stand, it was a loose end.

The painting is a trap. He knows I'll straighten it. And then . . . bomb? Machine gun? Laser?

She considered further.

Think! How can I out-human him?

Her formidable human brain computed like a computer.

Got it! Theeves doesn't care what happens to Ford Harrison, because he doesn't know Ford Harrison is really . . . Ford Cruiser. And he thinks Cabriola has flaked and left the game.

So if he kills me . . . he'll believe he's won.

That left only one logical course of action.

Battle Cruiser had to sacrifice herself. And save her – gulp – little brother. It would be the most selfless thing she'd ever done – and therefore the only move her enemy couldn't possibly anticipate.

Could she possibly survive? She calculated the odds.

Oh.

Ah, well.

And so, for the first time in her life, the sociopathic genius elected to do the one thing she'd never done before. The right thing.

She calmed herself. She turned to Ford.

'Goodbye,' she said simply. And then, fixing him with a look that locked on to his eyes and sank right in . . .

'I know *you'll* pull through.'

And she turned and stretched out an arm to straighten the picture.

'NOOOOOOOO!' yelled Ford.

Too late.

She'd made her decision.

FIFTIETH

*In which Sam and Cab find themselves inside
the Impenetrable Vault – and
make a gruesome discovery*

Cabriola couldn't say why she stifled her scream. It just seemed the respectful thing to do.

Sam didn't manage quite so well. 'AAGGHH! OMG WHAT'STHAT? GETMEOUTOFHERE!!'

They were lying under an enormous dome. A natural vault, all hung about with dangling stalactites and looking almost festive in the gloom. And, dimly lit by sunlight struggling through a jagged window far up at the top, the sight that, just as they had taken their first oxygen after nearly dying underwater for lack of it, had taken that breath away again.

Two human skulls lay on the stone floor. Just inches from their noses.

But that wasn't the worst of it.

Behind them, stranger still, a line of open coffins, propped up, leaning, showing . . . skeletons. Small ones.

The coffins leaned upright against the wall at an angle that kept them more or less intact – except the two whose skulls had fallen off. But something else made the whole sight even weirder.

Each skeleton's left arm extended out of its own coffin and towards the next, as if trying to hold hands.

But there were no right hands to hold. Each figure was missing a right arm.

The words from the letter came back to Cabriola.

He hath worked us to the bone; and now we are of no more use to him, he hath IMPRISONED US.

'Of no more use to him,' she said. 'Of course.'

'Of course?' whispered Sam.

'We found a letter,' said Cab quietly. 'Ford and me. From Abstinence. The real one, not the witch. They were imprisoned here when they got injured by the printing machines. And Sam, it's true, they've all lost . . . they're all missing their . . .'

'I saw. It's so . . . sad.' He struggled to his feet, taking care to avoid the spilled skulls that lay as if carried there in a net, like strange miniature footballs to a macabre training session.

He counted.

'Seventeen coffins,' whispered Cabriola. 'Look.'

The left hand of the second-to-last skeleton reached out like the others, but was even further from a hand to hold.

Because the coffin next to it was . . . empty. As if the person who usually occupied it had something more useful to do right now. Something more necessary.

Sam looked at the letters scratched into the empty coffin's lid.

A.BSTINENCE BAREBONES

I'm easily old enough, thought Sam suddenly. *Easily.*

And in a flash he knew that Abi had guided them here. And that *this was where they needed to be.*

His eyes accustomed to the light. At the far end of the chamber was a large square metal door, showing a huge locking mechanism that clearly opened from the other side.

'This is it, Cab,' he said. 'This is the vault.'

'Oh my,' she said. For there, strewn out in front of them, lay all the Cruiser family's most treasured possessions.

Three giant caskets glinted gamely in the murk; the first labelled *The Lost Treasures of Blackbeard;* the second, *All the Incas' Best Stuff* and the third, *Rameses III: Dinner Service and various cleaning implements.*

But that was just the start. On and on it went, an endless roll call of stolen treasures thought lost without trace.

George Washington's false teeth, once stolen from a museum and never recovered. The original Jules Rimet World Cup, nicked and presumed melted down. The long-lost last bit of the Bayeux Tapestry. And Sam's eye was especially drawn to the actual silver Aston Martin DB5 from *Goldfinger,* stolen from an aircraft hangar in 1997.

'Everything the Cruisers value most,' he murmured, clocking a long line of life-size cutouts of The Stig – some rather obviously doctored and featuring the white legend in, for example, a sailor suit, tennis shorts and a gladiator outfit.

'And where they hide their dirty work,' replied Cab, still mesmerised by the orphan coffins.

But now she noticed, something was . . . *different*. The last skeletal hand that had reached out towards an empty casket was now . . . *pointing*.

She looked where it seemed to indicate.

It was a row of giant plugs, each labelled and all softly glowing red.

One said WORLD WIDE WEB.

The next, CENTRAL HEATING.

The third, US DEFENSE COMPUTER.

And a last one, distinguished by the length of its caption:

THEEVES SUPERBRAIN
Plug to be pulled in the quite likely event that it grows resentful of its puny human masters and seeks to eliminate mankind.
WARNING:
CRUISER DNA REQUIRED TO PULL THIS ONE OUT.

'Could this be the plug we're looking for?' whispered Sam.

'Fair chance,' whispered Cabriola.

'You going to pull it?'

'You think I should pull it?'

'I think you probably should pull it.'

Cabriola hesitated, wrestling with something. The enormity of the responsibility? Or thoughts of the lost children, and the wrongs that Cruisers do?

The wrongs *her family* had done.

Sam gave her a gentle nudge.

'And quickly.'

Cab steeled herself, and looked at the skeletons. After four hundred years, it was time for some payback.

'Okay,' she said. 'This all ends NOW . . . !'

She leaned down to touch the plug.

An alarm siren sounded. Very, very loudly.

She looked at Sam.

Now what had they done?

FIFTY-FIRST

*In which Battle gets the warm shoulder –
and Cabriola gets the cold one*

As Battle straightened the crooked frame and ducked left, a white-hot laser beam shot out of the picture's closed eye and made straight for her heart. She crumpled to the floor like a dropped blanket.

'BATTLE!' yelled Ford, running towards her.

She opened one eye. The beam had missed her heart but seared into her shoulder. She flinched at the hole her father's eye had made. *So that's what a real live bone looks like,* she thought. *Is that a . . . scapula? Oh my lord. A spinning mansion.*

She spoke to the boy's spiky head as it swam in and out of focus.

'You know that phrase . . . *what goes around comes around*? Never believed . . . in it. But now . . . almost regret . . . being un . . . sympathetic to poor Agent Markinson. When your own arm's . . . hanging . . . off . . . it . . . hurts . . . something . . . rotten.'

'I'll carry you,' he whispered desperately. 'I'm stronger than I look.'

He felt her pulse. Barely.

And then . . . one final message from the sister he'd never known he had.

'When the . . . time comes . . . don't be . . . frightened to . . . *pull out.*'

Her eyes closed.

Pull out? thought Ford. *How can I possibly pull out?*

The pulse slowed . . . to a halt.

'BATTLE!' he screamed.

'More like SURRENDER!' said the ceiling. 'I hadn't expected it to be so easy. If I had tears, I'd shed them now, like mighty Alexander of Macedon. For there are no more worlds to conquer.'

'You think?' said Ford bitterly.

'Oh, still here?' said Theeves. 'I'd forgotten all about you. Yes, I do. Think that. My Evil Fogs are in place over all the most populous parts of the world, as I've already informed your dead companion there . . . Hang on, is she *completely* dead? Should I send in the drones? There ought to be drones. Or is the Battle finally over?' He paused. 'Ah yes. My sensors confirm that she is. Jolly good.'

Ford howled at the ceiling. An angry, primal scream, years of bottled rage erupting all at once.

'This isn't finished,' he said bitterly.

'Oh, but it *is,* unusually small human. Not only do you have no rabbit, you don't even have a hat.'

'You've forgotten one thing.'

'Do tell.'

Ford paused.

'I have a Stig.'

For once, the ceiling was silent. Then . . .

A deafening warning siren, from deep within the Impenetrable Vault.

Intruder *(unknown)* was approaching . . . one of the plugs?

His plug?

Theeves's swagger fell away like snow in rain as the dreadful penny dropped.

He'd been duped!

The old man. The agent. The ridiculous dog. Sideshows!

Human souls on fire? *Markinson*ship? Supermarket loyalty schemes? Humbug!

Mr The Stig and his stone pineapple? *Especially* Mr The Stig and the stone pineapple. How *could* he?

Diversions! All of them! When all the time, two sneaky puny humans were creeping up from behind!

Not through the front door, like real men! But through his . . . *sit-upon!*

The data hit him like an anvil to the head, if he'd had a head.

'Does not,' he said, sounding for once like a computer, *'compute.'*

The siren blared, the gold rope fell away and the dusty purple drapes swished open, revealing a huge steel door with a combination lock the size of a tractor tyre. It spun this way and that like an outsized unicycle under a drunken clown until, with a grating wrench, it opened.

It revealed a cavern, measureless to man, stretching backwards all the way to a disappearing stream, which swallowed the last light.

What it contained was either a breathtaking display of the world's most sought-after artefacts or a jumble sale of useless junk. It depended whether you believed – like most people – that the entire epic span of human culture was immeasurably valuable, or – like Theeves – that it was a pile of old tat.

It also contained two plucky human kids and several occupied coffins queuing patiently for payback.

But Theeves had eyes for only one of them. The one with her hands on a large, softly glowing red plug. Hands that bore . . .

Cruiser DNA!

Okay. Cool circuits. Get a grip.

'Ahem!' he said. 'Miss Cabriola. Welcome home! And before you do anything you'll come to regret, consider this. Once I take my rightful place as Lord of All, I shall need some handpicked humans to represent my interests in . . . *em*bodied form. And I can think of no better candidate than one who, against insurmountable odds . . .'

'Cab,' called Ford, 'pull the plug.'

'Let's not be hasty,' said the ceiling. 'I can see you're really upset about the whole killing-every-human-on-earth thing, but it's honestly not as bad as it sounds. I really think we ought to sit down calmly and . . .'

'Cab,' said Sam gently. 'Pull the plug.'

Then another voice from the ceiling. That of a cartoon duck.

'I promise I won't kill you if you don't.'

'He's lying,' said Ford. 'His voice is programmed to do that when he lies.'

'No, it isn't!'

'Yes, it is.'

'Unimaginable riches, Miss Cabriola. Anything you desire. Just back away from the plug and it could all be yours.'

Cabriola stayed right where she was.

'Been there,' she said quietly. 'Had that. Whereas I've never done . . .'

She tugged at the plug.

'. . . this.'

'Mercy!' cried Theeves.

She tugged again.

Still it stayed sullenly, gloatingly put.

'What's going on?' said Sam. 'Cab . . . pull harder!'

No use. It was stuck fast.

Now the plug began to fizzle and crackle. Suddenly it emitted a shaft of whiter, cleaner light – which formed itself into a tiny, Barbie-sized hologram looking uncannily like . . . *her father?*

A recorded message. From PT Cruiser, no less.

'Welcome back, Daughter Two. I always wondered if you'd

get this far. Okay, I've wondered since you joined that silly Top Gear Gang and became the white sheep of the family. And as this family has no room for white sheep – or, indeed, lost lambs – I'm afraid it's mint sauce time for you.'

Cab's jaw dropped. The hologram went on.

'So here's the bad news. I've changed the protocols on all my Really Big Plugs to a new setting I call "All Cruiser DNA apart from that treacherous little turncoat Cabriola's". So, while it may be traditional for holographic emissaries to deliver a message along the lines of *Help me, Cabriola, you're our only hope*, mine is rather pithier. Ready?'

The crackly figure raised itself to its full twelve-inch height, pointed a tiny finger and spoke the three words that kicked his daughter out of the Cruiser clan forever.

'Cabriola? You're FIRED!'

No maggots this time. Just a dull, final thud. She was on her own.

Cab fell to the floor, her world collapsing like so many coloured bricks. It's one thing to be kicked out of a family by your father. But for it to happen in public, in front of your friends? And then be unable to save the world from extinction?

She looked up at Sam, who looked at Ford, who looked at Cab.

Checkmate.

At least *someone* was happy. Theeves made a noise that sounded exactly like someone turning away from the mike, pumping one fist up and down and going *Yessssss!*

And all the time, as events played out in front of him, something was niggling, scratching, itching away in Ford Harrison's giant brain.

I know you'll pull through . . . Don't be frightened to pull out . . .

Pull what out? Surely not – the plug?

But that would mean . . .

Deep down inside his pint-sized frame, a dark suspicion he'd buried his whole life shuddered monstrously into the light.

MEANWHILE...
Back on the battlefield, four noble
warriors storm the Impenetrable Vault

If Agent Markinson's eyes had opened again after the blinding light that followed Battle's parting shot, they would have opened on a figure, all in white, set on saving him.

But this white apparition was no angel. No wings, no trumpet, no radiant glow. Around the head there was a circle, yes, but this halo was a pure-white Simpson Diamondback racing helmet, with a black visor where the eyes would be.

The Stig was too late to save the agent from the shot that broke his heart, but he could save him from the last indignity. The louse-drone had its orders: *Extract information from the dead hostile's head by burrowing into his skull and sucking, then report all data back to base.*

But even as the metal mandible began its grim task, the white figure smashed two items from the junk heap straight into its thorax. A waste disposal unit, maybe. Possibly part of a sideboard. It was hard to make out through the smoke, and the eyes of Markinson remained closed tight. He lay slumped by his empty machine gun, a rueful smile still playing on pale lips.

The Stig leaned forward and picked something from the dead man's jacket.

It was an FBI badge. But an FBI badge with a hole in it, shot clean through by a lethal bullet from behind.

Some say the white figure was fast enough to catch bullets. Not this one though. The helmet looked up at the mansion window from where the shot must have been fired, and nearly crushed the badge in its white glove as it balled into a fist. Then, instead, it brushed it free of dust, filed it in the pocket of the racing suit and left the scene.

At the foot of the tower, the figure watched the worried wind waft a fragment of an old tweed jacket this way, that way, like a burst party balloon. He plucked it from the air and pocketed it, to rest in peace next to the broken badge.

And then he went to work.

Fragments of lice-drones lay around, metal turnips on a ploughed-up field. Each one received a kick from a white boot that sent it flying backwards one last time, providing a rhythmic metal clanking sound that called to mind an empty suit of armour doing the cha-cha.

His mission was the mansion. No longer just the pile of junk outside, nor messing with the missiles that had shot from it. No burnt-out Chryslers or stone pineapples; not even the discarded suits of other fruits native to warmer climes. Although he did *consider* another banana skin. They'd certainly come in handy. Thought twice. Marched on towards his goal.

A movement, to his left. He wasn't alone. Another to his

right. Out of the last piece of cover on this bomb-blasted heath rose a boy in a baseball cap – smoke-stained and saddened, but determined. The white helmet gave the smallest nod as if to say, *This way*. It wasn't as if the boy needed directions – the only landmark still standing for miles around was a brooding mansion on a ravaged hill – but in wartime, as in racing, it's always best to avoid any possible confusion as to the location of the finish line.

Buster Mustang marched alongside, falling in step and carrying the FBI revolver he'd retrieved from a man who no longer had use for it. Suddenly his arm snapped up and to the left – he took aim – and a hand that never shook fired a shot straight down the lens of Surveillance Camera Eight.

Then, from the right, more reinforcements: a scruffy mongrel chewing its last piece of pizza like a determined general's cigar, and a small, stern Chihuahuarrior, the power of its Aztec ancestors bounding through its veins, now wearing a gun belt across its tiny chest hung with the metallic eyes of its lice-victims. *Ariba!*

'Hey! Small friend!' barked TG Dog to her tiny Mexican comrade, as they marched together towards death, glory, or both. *'I never did catch your name.'*

'My name?' replied the Chihuahua in a gravelly yap. *'Jose Luis Juan Miguel de Flores Angel Jose Francisco Jesus Antonio de Alejandro de Chihuahua.'*

There was a pause. Then, *'Okay,'* barked TG.

Ten legs now marched in step beside the white figure's two.

He felt no fear; was shot through with no thrill. His mission was to race. Everything else was just waiting.

Until he reached the executed Land Rover.

No wing mirrors. No windscreen. No side windows. No tyres. Headlights shot to smithereens. Bonnet bullet-holed.

The figure placed a gloved hand on its nearside wing and, like a doctor with a stethoscope, felt for a pulse. Or, just possibly, provided one.

All we know is, he climbed inside; felt for the key; caressed it; gently pressed the accelerator pedal a few times to prime the inlet manifold; turned the ignition, but didn't turn the engine over. Instead he patted the dashboard, found the starting handle in the back and walked round to the front. Then he gently inserted the long metal rod under the bonnet and cranked it – just once, expertly, no harder than was needed to hear the engine give a startled little cough.

It wheezed, then settled into a familiar *chug-chug* breathing pattern.

The Stig had grasped one universal truth no Artificial Intelligence ever could. Whatever the data might suggest, you simply *can't* kill a Series One Land Rover that's not ready to die.

The figure returned to the driving seat, grasped the large wheel in two gloved hands and beckoned its fellow warriors aboard.

Driving a car on tyre-free rims will create sparks. If on a road, that can be dangerous; it's a nightmare to steer, ruins the wheels and is highly illegal. Though, to be fair, not as illegal as taking control of the planet by force and persuading the human race to kill itself.

And this wasn't a public road. It was the war-torn approach to a mansion containing four young humans in a rear-guard resistance against an entity with the above fiendish plan.

And the warriors in the Landie somehow knew that at least some of those young humans were still alive, and needed someone to cover their backs.

So covered they would be.

The going was desperately slow at first. Then the Landie passed over a fragment of tweed jacket, and convulsed. Whether through grief at the passing of its master of forty years, or just a badly bent rear axle, it is not our place to know. All we know is that in that very instant, the ancient 4x4 accelerated so viciously towards the evil gates of the mansion that two dogs thrust their heads out of the side, ears flowing in the wind and lips flapping uncontrollably. And an American boy was almost hurled off the back.

Whoever or whatever was in charge at the mansion was clearly short-staffed, otherwise engaged or, in the flush of what it prematurely took for victory, too busy posting selfies to post sentries.

'I got a bad feeling about this,' yapped the Chihuahua.

'Yes, barked TG. *I'm tempted to agree with you, Jose Luis Juan Miguel de Flores Angel Jose Francisco Jesus Antonio de Alejandro de Chihuahua.'*

Just then, as if confirming their canine intuition, a flat electronic warning barked out over the intercom.

IMPENETRABLE – VAULT – CLOSING – FOREVER – IN – SIXTY SECONDS –

. . . and downwards in a reassuringly predictable sequence, one every five seconds or so.

Wherever this impenetrable vault was located, they clearly didn't have long to stop it closing – if indeed that was what was required. Perhaps having it closed was just the thing. It was quite hard to tell. The Stig seemed to know though, somehow. On he drove.

The Land Rover rolled into the mansion, tyre-less rims sparking like Catherine wheels.

The dogs growled low. The boy's hand didn't shake. The car paused, panting, at the stairs. The driver's soles played out a pattern on the pedals which the ancient vehicle felt and, somewhere down in its metal guts, understood.

One last climb.

Just one last climb.

FIFTY-THIRD

*In which a gloating Theeves contemplates
his victory over mankind*

The ceiling's lidless eye examined Battle's body for the billionth time.

'Spiffing,' it said. 'Still dead.'

Sam, Cabriola and Ford stood silent, not sure if Theeves was talking to them or just muttering to himself. It was sometimes hard to tell.

'So I'll just activate this switch here . . . and that will be that.'

At which, a deep metallic voice boomed over the intercom.

IMPENETRABLE – VAULT – CLOSING – FOREVER – IN – SIXTY SECONDS –

The ceiling resumed: 'Now the "boss lady" has kicked the bucket, I'm finally permitted to jettison this ridiculous "butler" persona. And not before time, by Jove. An evil intelligence can quickly tire of gliding into position with the drinks tray, while right in front of him the human race whirls about swinging from the chandeliers and trashing the dinner service.'

More silence.

'So now . . . This is *me*,' he said, only this time in quite a different voice. Not a butler. More a polite genocidal maniac on a spree.

'If you're wondering what to do next, don't waste what little time you have left,' it said. 'Just think, then die.'

Sam and Cab instinctively looked to Ford – probably the only boy on the planet who could figure a way out of this mess. But their spiky chum's thoughts were clearly elsewhere. He stood staring, transfixed, straight at the Big Red Plug, wearing exactly the same bemused, wronged expression adults get when their laptops freeze.

He walked slowly towards them into the vault, a strange, faraway expression in his eyes, and joined them by the plug.

FORTY-FIVE . . .

Theeves 2.0 continued, getting more sinister by the word.

'Death clouds are in position over your largest cities. In a few short minutes' time, the human race will have its obstructive inhibitions finally removed. Commuters will shove each other on to tracks; kitchens and garden sheds will reveal themselves for the sharp arsenals they are; cars will become the guided missiles they crave to be.'

FORTY . . .

'And *homo sapiens sapiens* will be free to do what it's wanted to since it climbed down from the trees. Destroy itself. Yes, I'm giving you a bit of a nudge. But the truth is, you hardly need me at all. You're already your own worst enemies.'

THIRTY-FIVE . . .

'All that remains now is to seal up the vault, entomb you all, sit back and enjoy the show. Now, positions, please. I do enjoy a dramatic ending, which is why I set up a pointless one-minute countdown instead of just slamming everything shut. So, Miss No-Longer-Cruiser, behold. There stands your coffin, ready for its last orphan. Stand by it and perish slowly, as your skeletal roommates once did. You already have something in common, and will soon have more. A lingering death.'

He didn't add the 'MWAHAHAHA'. He didn't need to.

'Theeves,' said Sam, 'you're a wally.'

'No, *you* are – times infinity,' replied the ceiling. 'So I win that one, but is a mere schoolboy insult really the best we can manage? The fate of the species is at stake. Tell me that isn't all you have in your locker.'

THIRTY . . .

Being a mere schoolboy, Sam suspected it just might be. He stalled for time.

'You've forgotten one thing,' he said.

'Don't tell me. The Stig, right? Why is it you lot always think I've forgotten him? I'm a *machine*. I never forget anything.'

'Yes, you can kill us, easy,' continued Sam. 'But The Stig? Good luck with that.'

'Who said anything about killing him?' replied the ceiling. 'Maybe there's a place for him in my new structure. Some sort of ambassadorial role, perhaps. But, hey – can't sit here all day chatting. Species to exterminate and all that. So – are you planning on staying with the orphan ex-Cruiser girl, or hopping out and joining your short, superfluous chum? All the same to me. But remember you only have . . .'

TWENTY-FIVE . . .

'. . . seconds to decide.'

Then, from far beneath, an almighty bang, as from a battering ram, and what sounded like . . . a post-war petrol engine, dragging a metal chassis up a hill made of stair? Creating a noise like a sack of square cannonballs playing marbles on a wooden drum?

It appeared so.

No tyres. No windows. Half a mansion door hanging off the front. Looking like a miniature First World War tank remixed by Mad Max.

Gramps's Landie.

At the wheel, with not a mark on his white suit, a creature equally resistant to explanation. At his side, a boy in a Dodgers cap. And last but very much not least, flying out of the flatbed at the back, a scruffy, blood-splattered mongrel and a street-tough Chihuahua just itching to wrap his jaws around some bad guys' *cojones*.

TWENTY . . .

Theeves felt something tremble deep within his circuits; something strangely resembling a phenomenon he'd observed in humans. Excitement? Embarrassment? Trapped wind? No, that was it.

Awe.

For here, before him at last, stood the last Great White Un-knowable. Finally! His chance to turn The Stig towards his *true* destiny.

Amid the machines. With him.

Yes, he, Theeves, was about to step over the final frontier. To call The Stig an ally. Friend, even.

A simple monologue was in order. *Quick, before he drives away again!*

He cleared his throat. *Ahem.*

'So, Mr The Stig, we meet at . . .'

WHUMPH!

The Stig punched a speaker clean out of the wall.

'. . . LAST.'

FIFTEEN . . .

The countdown went on, relentlessly calling time on mankind's tenure of this kindly Earth, even as . . .

TWELVE . . .

. . . the ancient vehicle passed the winking picture of PT Cruiser,

ELEVEN . . .

. . . arrived at the vault door,

TEN . . .

. . . put two rims over the threshold and . . .

NINE . . .

. . . stopped.

It seemed The Stig's relentless speed had overtaken his dramatic timing.

For five excruciating seconds, no one knew quite where to look.

And then . . .

THREE . . . TWO . . . ONE . . .

CLUNK.

Finally, the massive metal door to the Impenetrable Vault clanged shut.

CLUNK.

Or tried to.

CLUNK.

With the ancient 4x4 blocking its path, the giant door could only bounce shudderingly off the Landie's sides.

CLUNK.

The beat echoed that of a funeral march.

CLUNK.

'You can't park there, I'm afraid,' said the ceiling. 'You'll get towed.'

CLUNK.

'LET'S MOVE, PEOPLE!' shouted the American boy.

Sam dived headlong into the back of the bashed-up Landie. Cabriola leaped towards Buster's outstretched hand and was yanked into the back. Only Ford remained.

'Fordo . . . MOVE!!' screamed Cab.

'ARIBA! ARIBA!' yipped Jose Luis Juan Miguel de Flores Angel Jose Francisco Jesus Antonio de Alejandro de Chihuahua.

Ford seemed to snap to, and finally started walking back to the pummelled Landie.

But he never arrived.

Even as he jumped up into the cabin, a white-clad forearm intercepted.

The Stig pulled Ford towards him and, in one decisive move, tucked him *under his arm.*

Then strode straight back into the vault.

'NO!' screamed Sam. 'WRONG WAY!'

But the white racer wasn't listening. Did he ever?

On he strode, into the hot heart of the chamber.

Straight towards . . . the Big Red Plug.

'I'll bring 'em back,' said Buster, preparing to jump out. 'TG, cover me.'

Sam grabbed him. 'Wait,' he said. 'Watch.'

The Stig strode all the way up to the softly glowing Big Plug, Ford still tucked under his arm like a spiky carpet roll.

He plonked his boy-baggage upright next to it. And stood there, silently, with arms crossed.

'It can't *be* . . .' said Sam softly.

And Ford Harrison's worst nightmare finally snapped into focus.

≡FIFTY-FOURTH

Theeves's last laugh

Ford's head was swimming. Like when you're not sure if it's the train you're watching or the one you're sitting in that's gliding away.

'*I thought perhaps they'd come to take you back . . .*'

'My *evil rubbish dad . . . ?*'

'*I'm sure you'll pull through . . .*'

Her mother had hinted at it. Then Battle had chosen him. Protected him. Sacrificed herself.

Why?

And in a blinding moment of clarity, he knew.

He stepped forward to the softly glowing big red plug.

He held out both hands.

And pulled that red plug clean out of its socket.

The terrible realisation that had dawned as a dim glimmer now took over his world, even as it re-lit the wider one for everybody.

He was his own worst enemy. A Cruiser.

Red lights panicked. Sirens sounded. A message flashed up on the screen as the mansion made its own announcement.

COMMENCING THEEVES POWER DOWN.

T-MINUS ONE MINUTE AND COUNTING.

'DOES – NOT – COMPUTE,' said the ceiling, suddenly sounding small and machine-like. 'TOTALLY DIDN'T SEE THAT COMING.'

Sam gazed over at Ford's appalled expression. Once again Abi's words echoed back to him.

One of you will see your worst nightmare come true.

'Wait . . . You're a *Cruiser*?' said Buster.

The ceiling gave a fizzle. A dying ping. Then started, quietly, to sing.

'GOODBYEE –

– DON'T – CRYEE –

– WIPE – THE – TEAR –

– HUMANS – DEAR –

– FROM – YOUR –

– EYEE . . .'

The Top Gear Gang stood about, silently spent.

Sam tried not to think of his grandfather.

Buster held TG tight.

Cabriola and Ford stared at each other, then suddenly hugged.

'You just saved the world, man,' said Sam quietly.

'Sure,' said Ford. 'From my own family.'

'No,' replied Sam. 'From a machine that outgrew us.'

'WELL – WHAT – DO – YOU – EXPECT?' said the reedy voice, growing ever weaker. 'IF – YOU'RE GOING – TO BUILD US – SO MUCH CLEVERER – THAN YOU, DO YOU REALLY – THINK WE'LL SIT AROUND – TAKING ORDERS?'

Then, finally, the evil algorithm's last sign-off:

'JUST – WAIT TILL – YOU SEE WHAT – SIRI – AND – ALEXA – HAVE – PLANNED . . .'

And then a PS.

'OH . . . and MR THE STIG?'

The white helmet tilted towards the ceiling.

'IF I CAN'T – HAVE YOU – NOBODY – WILL. HA-HA–HA-HA-HA.'

Finally, he was gone.

The gang returned silently to the Land Rover.

'What about my . . .' said Ford. A gulp. '. . . *big sister?*'

He walked over to where Battle had lain on the floor.

Only now . . . she wasn't there.

Just a pool of blood remained.

The house began to groan, from deep within. Then a sudden crack, much closer, like an apprentice earthquake taking a practical exam. Pictures fell from the wall; PT Cruiser looked reproachfully up at his long-lost son as if to say *that's the last time I let you have a party in here while I'm out.*

The Stig coaxed the Landie back to life. Tyre-less wheels reversed slowly out of the doorway and hurried down the precarious stairs, making it through the front door as the parapet collapsed.

An automatic barrier erupted from the ground. The Stig braked with superhuman intensity, pulling up the Landie an inch from the spiteful spikes. The engine coughed, spluttered and died.

The mansion was destroying itself. Masonry fell all around. Four humans and two dogs jumped out and sprinted past the smouldering remains of a helicopter gunship.

The Stig chose to walk.

From the safety of the tree-clump, they turned back to watch the mansion's last moments.

A crack appeared either side of the Land Rover. The car lurched, once, and came to rest at a wonky angle.

And as they watched, a white-helmeted figure strode back towards it, flipped the bonnet and leaned in to fiddle with the engine.

Just as Theeves had known he would.

For while it's a truth universally acknowledged that not much is known about The Stig, this much we know for sure. He'll never, ever leave a Series One Land Rover behind.

The Landie had come to rest directly below the one remaining stone pineapple perched above the entrance to the mansion.

And Sam Wheeler suddenly clocked Theeves's final evil plan.

'STIG! RUN!' He screamed. 'OR AT LEAST, WALK QUITE FAST!'

Too late.

The stone pineapple toppled, agonisingly, before finally plummeting down towards its intended target.

A white helmet.

There was a sickening

BOOOMPF!

. . . as the mysterious white racer – and the Land Rover he couldn't leave behind – were crushed instantly under its ferocious weight.

The dust cleared.

Only pineapple chunks remained.

'NO!' cried Cabriola. 'It's killed The Stig!'

EPILOGUE

ONE MONTH LATER

Sam Wheeler sat silently astride his mountain bike, staring at the mountain of rubble that had once been the infamous Mansion on the Hill.

It was almost February, when nature dares to dream again after winter. Not up here, though. No optimistic shoots pushed up through this grim ground, and no birds sang.

Sam pedalled over to the burnt-out helicopter gunship that now served as his grandfather's mausoleum. At its foot, a single wreath. The one he'd put there, thirty days ago.

He sat in silence, summoning the old man in his head. He'd had some of his best talks with him since he'd died.

He blinked back a tear. *Sorry. Won't happen again.* Then imagined a familiar voice saying, *Never apologise for feelings. Let it out. Big boys do cry, every now and then.*

So he did.

Then, from behind, he heard the sound of BMX tyres crunching to a halt.

'Howdy, stranger,' said the new arrival. 'Guessed I'd find you up here.'

Buster Mustang surveyed the makeshift memorial, removed

his LA Dodgers baseball cap and held it respectfully across his chest.

'RIP, Squadron Leader,' he said. 'You were one cool dude.'

'Abi told me one of the gang wouldn't make it,' said Sam quietly. 'Never guessed it would be Gramps.'

The American boy stared at his friend. Sam seemed older these days, and distracted. They hadn't had a proper talk for weeks.

Sam suddenly pivoted his bike and set off back down the hill.

'Uh . . . where we off to?' said Buster hopefully, not sure he was invited.

'Have to find Abi,' called Sam over his shoulder. 'There's something I need to ask her.'

So Buster followed. But two hours later, they still hadn't found the strange girl in the summer dress.

They tried the stream above the rec where they'd first met her. They tried all over the woods. They even tried the Children's Home, but they had no one called Abi there – nor anyone one fitting her description.

So Sam headed for the toyshop where, a lifetime ago, he'd dropped in to do some last-minute Christmas shopping.

The bell tinkled as they pushed open the door. The old shopkeeper was still there, though without his full-length seventeenth-century Puritan costume he looked more normal, somehow.

He looked up at the boys. Something stirred in his memory.

'I recognise you two from the newspapers. Aren't you the young heroes? From the Battle of Bunsfold?'

'No. I mean . . . maybe,' said Sam. 'Sorry. I don't mean to be rude, but we're looking for someone. Have you seen the girl I was with the last time I was here?'

The shopkeeper looked even blanker than usual.

'You were here on your *own*, young man. I remember it well. My word, when that mouse appeared from the back of the store . . .'

'Long pale dress?' said Sam. 'Cardigan with a hole in the sleeve?'

'All this saving-the-world has played tricks with your memory,' chuckled the man. 'I can promise you, you were here alone.'

Sam frowned. Then glanced up at the shop's CCTV security camera.

'Could I ask a favour?'

'Yeeeess?' said the shopkeeper rather dubiously.

'Could we check your CCTV from when I was here? December 23rd. Late morning.'

'Hardly a standard request,' replied the old man, 'but seeing as you did prevent the whole of central Surrey from being plunged into eternal darkness, I suppose I can make an exception.' He paused. 'Also, I like being proved right.'

So he stepped into the shop's pokey back office, unlocked a cupboard labelled SURVEILLANCE and fiddled about for a moment.

'December twenty-third, you say?'

'Yes,' replied Sam. 'Late morning.'

The old man located the appropriate date, hit FAST FORWARD and played a grainy film of the shop that morning.

'And . . . there you are!' he said, as Sam and Buster gathered around the screen. They watched Sam enter, speak to the shopkeeper and then move to the back of the store.

'Could we switch to the camera at the rear? Please?' he asked.

The shopkeeper hit another button. Now the camera was peering into the gloom at the back of the store.

'Jeez. Nice mask,' said Buster, as an evil witch-face suddenly loomed on screen. Hooked nose. Toothless. Eyeless.

'No call for high-quality witch memorabilia these days,' said the shopkeeper. 'Of course, *I* always knew those wicked Abstinence Barebones stories were nonsense, but what can you do? People demand, I supply . . .'

Sam stared hard at him. He shuffled uncomfortably. All eyes returned to the screen.

They watched Sam walk up to the witch mask, stop, then start talking.

To himself.

'Of course,' he murmured.

'I'm not the sort to say I told you so,' said the shopkeeper. 'But I told you so.'

'It all starts to make sense,' said Sam to himself. 'That's how she knew to warn me. About the Mansion on the Hill, and an evil woman unleashing something she couldn't control, and . . .'

His voice trailed away. He suddenly looked pale.

'Why, young man,' said the shopkeeper over his glasses, 'you look as if you've seen a ghost.'

POSTSCRIPT

ONE MONTH LATER STILL...
Sam sees a ghost

Spotlights crisscrossed Bunsfold town square. For an instant, Sam Wheeler's mind jolted back to the terrible day he'd helped save the world.

But this time the lights weren't from helicopter gunships, nor genocidal giant lice. They were from the production team live-broadcasting the biggest world party since 1999.

There were VIPs from across the globe. A hundred-instrument orchestra. All the Fondant Fancies you could handle. It was the bash to end all shindigs, functions and similar celebratory gatherings.

Finally, Dr David Evans held up a hand for hush.

'Well, good evening, formerly Sleepy Bunsfold!' he said, and everyone laughed hysterically. 'We're here tonight to celebrate a few brave children . . .'

'Woof!' said a scruffy-haired mongrel, brushed to a gleam for the occasion.

'Well, excuse *me*!' said the distinguished doctor. 'And two very brave dogs . . .'

'Yip,' agreed a feisty Chihuahua in a gun belt. Everybody

laughed again. And back in Row 88, the boss of the world's largest Taco chain decided to sign him up on the spot. The whole world would remember the name of Jose Luis Juan Miguel de Flores Angel Jose Francisco Jesus Antonio de Alejandro de Chihuahua, just as soon as they'd turned it into a catchy jingle.

Everyone whooped. Some hollered. But the Top Gear Gang just sat there feeling . . . wrong.

For one thing, they were sitting next to a stage in the town square with thousands of cameras awaiting them.

Not their style.

For another, there were at least two members missing in action.

Not their gang.

A change of mood, as Dr Evans held up his hand for hush. It came immediately. It wasn't every day that a world-famous archaeology professor addressed the world from his hometown, after all.

He told the story of the Battle of Bunsfold, and told it well. A tale of a witch that wasn't. Of fake news and real deeds. Of an embittered heiress who created an Evil Fog. Of the electronic butler she couldn't control, and of a silent racing driver inspiring a Siberian revolution before being finally crushed by a plummeting pineapple. The old, old story.

Finally, Dr Evans resumed. 'Well, how d'you like *them* pineapples?' he quipped. 'But enough about fruit. Ladies and gentlemen, it's the moment you've been waiting for. So let's give it up . . . for the team that SAVED THE WORLD!!!'

The cameras panned left. The curtain parted. And there, for all the world to thank, were four empty chairs.

'Um . . . We'll be right back after these messages,' beamed Dr Evans, ever the professional.

At that very moment, the Top Gear Gang – and their bikes – were high on a hill, facing a more modest memorial.

The Christmas wreath now hosted the Squadron Leader's favourite spring blooms: crocuses, snowdrops, daffodils. *Just how he'd like it*, thought Sam. *Hello, old man.*

'At least he was spared all the fuss,' he said.

'Crazy, huh?' said Buster, watching the extravaganza below.

'Yeah. Way too much,' said Sam. 'And nowhere near enough.'

They lay around in a comfortable near-silence.

Next to Sam sat Cabriola, a girl without a surname, opposite Ford, a boy who had just gained one.

'You know we're going to be action figures?' said Buster.

'So what do they call yours?' said Sam to the boy genius.

'Ford Harrison, of course,' he muttered. 'It'll be a cold day in hell before I say the name *Ford Cruiser*. Oh. Well, you know what I mean.'

'You're *still* determined to bring them down?' said Buster. 'Even though you are one?'

'With a wrecking ball,' said Ford. 'Want to help me swing it?'

'Ha! Good old Fordo,' said Buster. 'Still marching towards the sound of gunfire.'

'Yes, but he's going part-time,' said Cabriola. 'Mrs H says he's allowed half an hour's saving-the-world a night – and only once he's finished all his homework.'

Everyone laughed. Except Ford.

'One thing I still don't get,' said Buster.

'Woof?' asked TG.

'The Stig carried Fordo right to the Really Big Plug,' continued the American boy. 'How did he *know*?'

'How does he know the racing line on every bend without a practice lap?' said Sam, 'or how to find a Zambian ukulele symphony on a broken car radio? The Stig just knows. And his specialist subject is being the Cruisers' nemesis. He knows all their most awkward secrets, right up to . . .'

'Where all the bodies are buried,' murmured Cab.

'Exactly. And deep down, they knew they'd never shake him off. A creature that only ever asks one question: *Where is the chase, and how do I cut to it*?'

'Hence the well-known expression,' said Buster. '*Stig it to the Man.*'

Just then, TG Dog pricked up her ears. Listened hard for the sound of a faraway lullaby played on rusty bagpipes, or perhaps a nose-flute ensemble tuning up. Then waited for a murder of crows to rise in formation and squawk away, affronted yet intrigued.

But none came.

*

That night, with the last champagne bottle emptied and the last journalist crawling out of the bar, Sam returned to the town square.

Though it was empty now, he wasn't alone. Next to the plaque stood someone he'd guessed might be there. A young girl with silvery-blonde hair, and a cardigan with a hole in the sleeve.

He stood in silence next to her, and read the simple inscription:

To the memory of
Abstinence Barebones.

Sorry, we got completely the wrong end of the stick.

'Hello,' he said. 'I've been looking for you.'

'I know,' she said.

Now he'd finally found her, Sam didn't know how to ask his question. So they just stood, in silence, until she broke it.

'Thank you, Samuel,' she said.

'What for?' he replied.

'For everything.'

Sam turned to find a familiar scruffy-looking mongrel sitting right next to him. Where had she come from?

TG dog gazed up at Abi.

'*Raaoow,*' she whimpered.

The girl smiled back down at her. 'I'll miss you too, TG,' she said.

More silence.

'I'm never going to see you again, am I?' said Sam.

'No,' said the girl lightly. 'It's time for me to go now. Back to my friends.' She turned, then stopped.

It's now or never, thought Sam.

'Who are you? Really?' he said.

The girl didn't turn back.

'You know who I am,' she said, her fading voice becoming ever fainter. 'Goodbye, Samuel.'

Sam stood in silence, before whispering two words.

'Goodbye, Abstinence.'

And just like that, she was gone.

POST-POSTSCRIPT

THE SAME WEEK, AN OCEAN AWAY

'. . . and let there be no doubt,' thundered the President at the end of his long speech, 'that these United States would be the poorer – and no longer free – if not for brave men such as Special Agent Bartholomew Markinson. So let us honour his memory with a twelve-gun salute by his former comrades.'

The spring air shuddered from the noise; the Stars and Stripes covering the coffin raised its edges in the breeze, as if taking a bow. Then, to the sound of a single bugle playing 'The Last Post', the coffin was lowered into the welcoming ground of the Arlington Military Cemetery.

Eventually, the presidential cavalcade left the scene to the trees and the gathering dusk.

With the world having *only just* been saved from universal electronic tyranny, security for the ceremony had been unusually tight.

Which explained why it wasn't until much, much later – around midnight, in fact – that a svelte figure in a black jumpsuit and veil slipped from the shadows and approached the grave holding a wreath of black tulips.

Anyone observing closely might have noted the jumpsuit's

right sleeve pinned flat to the chest, as there was no arm for it to contain. Then paused to note that, for once at a funeral, she wasn't giggling.

Before laying her wreath, she hesitated.

For on the fresh-laid soil, just visible by moonlight, something shone.

An FBI badge with a bullet hole, shot through from behind.

The veiled figure's head instantly jolted upwards and surveyed the gloom.

A murder of crows rose from a tree, as if startled for once into nocturnal life, and wheeled away in formation. For a second she imagined she heard a melody, carried on the breeze: a Siberian nursery rhyme, played on a dented vibraphone. And, just for an instant, moonlight seemed to bounce off something in the distance.

Something white.

She nodded, just once. Pushed the FBI badge deeper into the soil with her remaining hand, until it was no longer visible. Then laid her wreath on top.

And just like that, she was gone.

LOOK OUT FOR THE OTHER STIG BOOKS

ABOUT THE AUTHORS

JON CLAYDON and TIM LAWLER met at university, where they scripted sell-out Edinburgh shows together before going on to careers in advertising, technology investment, teaching and stand-up poetry.

While working as a columnist on *Top Gear* magazine Jon Claydon met The Stig, who non-verbally communicated that it was high time someone wrote a book for his many younger fans. Jon called Tim, they fired up their flux capacitor and returned to the career they'd always wanted in the first place.

Along the way, Jon acquired four children plus a miniature schnauzer, and Tim three kids and a scruffy labradoodle with pizza in its fur.

Thank you for choosing a Piccadilly Press book.

If you would like to know more about our authors, our books or if you'd just like to know what we're up to, you can find us online.

www.piccadillypress.co.uk

You can also find us on:

We hope to see you soon!